MYSTERY OF THE
PHANTOM HEIST

HARDY BOYS ADVENTURES

#2 *MYSTERY OF THE PHANTOM HEIST*

FRANKLIN W. DIXON

ALADDIN   New York London Toronto Sydney New Delhi

ALADDIN

An imprint of Simon & Schuster Children's Publishing Division
1230 Avenue of the Americas, New York, NY 10020
First Aladdin paperback edition February 2013
Copyright © 2013 by Simon & Schuster, Inc.
All rights reserved, including the right of reproduction in whole or in part in any form.
ALADDIN is a trademark of Simon & Schuster, Inc.,
and related logo is a registered trademark of Simon & Schuster, Inc.
THE HARDY BOYS MYSTERY STORIES, HARDY BOYS ADVENTURES,
and related logo are trademarks of Simon & Schuster, Inc.
Also available in an Aladdin hardcover edition.
For information about special discounts for bulk purchases, please contact Simon & Schuster
Special Sales at 1-866-506-1949 or business@simonandschuster.com.
The Simon & Schuster Speakers Bureau can bring authors to your live event.
For more information or to book an event contact the Simon & Schuster Speakers Bureau
at 1-866-248-3049 or visit our website at www.simonspeakers.com.
The text of this book was set in Adobe Caslon Pro.
Manufactured in the United States of America 1212 OFF
2 4 6 8 10 9 7 5 3 1
Library of Congress Control Number 2012953641
ISBN 978-1-4424-6586-2 (hc)
ISBN 978-1-4424-2237-7 (pbk)
ISBN 978-1-4424-2238-4 (eBook)

CONTENTS

KEYED UP 1

FRANK

"YOU'VE GOT TO SEE THIS, FRANK!" JOE said. "You too, Chet. It's totally sick."

Help, I thought as my brother held up his prized possession, a tablet, for the gazillionth time. Not another lame clip on YouTube!

It was the last thing I wanted to look at as we sat inside the swanky Peyton mansion. I wanted to check out the two slick cabin cruisers docked outside the bay window!

"Will you give us a break already, Joe?" I told him. "I think we've seen enough skateboarding squirrels and break-dancing babies to last a lifetime."

Our friend Chet Morton cracked a smile. "Yeah, but those rapping sock puppets you showed us before were pretty sick," he admitted. "Got any more of those?"

Joe shook his head. "Check it out—it's serious stuff," he said, practically shoving the tablet in our faces.

"You, serious?" I joked. "Since when?"

Joe knew what I meant. Our ages were only one year apart, but our personalities—worlds apart. Joe was always high-strung, fast-talking, and unpredictable. Me—I'm more the strong, silent type. At least that's what I like to think.

"Will you look at the clip already?" Joe urged. "I can't keep it on pause forever." He hadn't put down that fancy new tablet since he got it for his birthday. I couldn't really blame him. We couldn't have smartphones until we were in college, so the tablet was the next best thing. It surfed the Web, got e-mails— even took pictures and videos. Speaking of videos . . .

"Okay," I sighed. "But if I see one squirrel or sock puppet— it's over."

Chet and I leaned forward to watch the clip. There were no skateboarding squirrels or sock puppets—just a clerk at a fast-food take-out window, handing a paper bag to a customer. The clerk looked about sixteen or seventeen. The person behind the wheel had his back to the camera, which was probably being held by someone in the passenger seat.

"Bor-ing!" Chet sighed.

"Wait, here it comes," Joe said. He turned up the volume just as the clerk said, "Six dollars and seventy cents, please."

The driver reached out to pay. But then he yanked the lid off his jumbo cup and hurled what looked like a slushie all over the kid at the take-out window!

"Keep the change!" the driver cackled before zooming off. I could hear another voice snickering—probably the creep filming the whole thing.

I stared at the screen. "Definitely not cool," I said.

"And a perfectly good waste of a jumbo slushie," Chet joked.

"Not funny, Chet," Joe said with a frown.

"How did you find that clip, Joe?" I asked.

"Lonny, a guy in my math class, forwarded it to me," Joe explained. "Lonny was the poor clerk who got slushied."

"Did they ever find the guys who did it?" Chet asked.

Joe shook his head and said, "The burger place called the cops, but so far the slushie slinger's still on the loose."

"You mean it's a—cold case?" Chet joked. "Cold . . . slushie—get it?"

"That's about as funny as those skateboarding squirrels, Morton," I complained. "What we just saw was someone's idea of a dumb prank."

"Yeah, but whose?" Joe asked.

This time Chet heaved a big sigh. "Time out, you guys!" he said. "You promised your dad you were going to slow down the detective work, at least for now."

"Slow down?" Joe asked. "From something we've been doing since we were seven and eight? Not a chance, bud."

Of course, what Joe didn't mention was that we were one wrong move away from reform school. No one knew about the Deal except our family, the police, and our former principal—who had his own issues to deal with now!

"Yeah, but a promise is a promise," I said. "So put that thing away already, Joe."

"Before somebody comes in and sees it," Chet added.

"What would be so bad about that?" Joe asked.

"Because," Chet said, smiling, "surfing clips on YouTube isn't the thing to be doing in the parlor of one of the über-richest homes in Bayport."

Glancing around the posh room we were sitting in, I knew Chet got the über-rich part right.

"Check out the pool table, you guys," I said.

"As soon as I finish checking out those little beauties," Chet said, nodding toward a nearby table. On it was a silver platter filled with fancy frosted pastries.

"Don't even think of taking one," Joe said, pointing to a portrait hanging on the wall. "Not while he's watching us."

I studied the portrait in the heavy wooden frame. The subject was a middle-aged guy in a blue blazer and beige pants. His hair was dark, with streaks of gray, and he was holding a golf club. I figured he was Sanford T. Peyton, the owner of the house, the boats, and the pastries.

I didn't know much about him, just that when the multi-billionaire dude wasn't living large in Bayport with his wife and daughter, he was opening hotels all over the country and maybe the world. The guy was crazy rich. And right now, crazy late!

"We've been waiting in this room almost half an hour," I said as I glanced at the antique clock standing against the

4

wall. "Can someone please remind me why we're here?"

"Gladly!" Chet said. He stood up with a smug smile. "My friends, we are about to be interviewed by Sanford T. Peyton for the honor of working the hottest party of the decade—at least here in Bayport."

With that, Chet turned to another portrait hanging on the opposite wall. This one showed a teenage girl with light brown hair, wearing a white sundress and holding a Cavalier King Charles spaniel with huge eyes.

"His daughter Lindsay's Sweet Sixteen!" Chet declared, pointing to the portrait with a flourish.

"Cute," Joe said with a grin. "And I don't mean the dog."

Chet and Joe were definitely psyched about this party. Too bad I couldn't say the same for myself.

"You guys, we weren't good enough to be invited to Lindsay's Sweet Sixteen," I said. "So why should we work it?"

"Two words, my friend, two words," Chet said with a smile. "Food and—"

"Girls!" Joe blurted out.

"Got it!" I said with a smirk.

The only thing I knew about Lindsay was that she didn't go to Bayport High with Chet, Joe, and me. Which was no surprise.

"Most of the kids at this party will be from Bay Academy," I said, referring to the posh private school in Bayport. "And you know what they're like. Total snobs—"

Chet cleared his throat loudly as the door swung open. Joe

and I jumped up from our chairs as Sanford Peyton marched in, followed by his daughter, Lindsay. Walking briskly behind Lindsay was another girl of about the same age. She had long black hair, and her dark eyes were cast downward at her own tablet she was holding. As she glanced up, she threw me a quick smile. I caught myself smiling back.

Hmm, I thought, still smiling. *Maybe this job isn't such a bad idea.*

"Have a seat, boys," Sanford said as he sat behind his desk, facing us. Lindsay and the other girl stood behind Sanford, looking over his shoulders at us.

As we sat back down, I could see Sanford studying the applications we'd filled out.

"I see you all go to Bayport High," he said gruffly.

"Yes, sir," I said.

"Daddy, they're cute, but not gladiator material," Lindsay cut in.

The three of us stared at Lindsay.

"Say what?" Joe said under his breath.

"Gladiators?" Chet said. "I thought you needed waiters. You know, to pass around the pigs in blankets."

"There will be no pigs in blankets at this party, boys," Sanford said.

"What kind of a party has no pigs in blankets?" Chet asked.

"Daddy." Lindsay sighed as she checked out her manicure. "Just explain."

Sanford folded his hands on the desk.

"You see, boys," he said, "the theme of Lindsay's Sweet Sixteen is No Place Like Rome. Four strong young men dressed as gladiators accompany Lindsay into the hall as she makes her grand entrance."

"You mean Empress Lindsay," Lindsay emphasized. "And the gladiators will be carrying me on a throne designed just for the occasion."

Joe, Chet, and I stared at Lindsay as she flipped her hair over her shoulder. Was she serious?

"Got it, I think," Joe said. "But you'll still need waiters, right?"

"For sure," Lindsay replied. She turned to the girl with the tablet and said, "Sierra, make sure you get the music I want for my grand entrance."

"'Hotter Than Vesuvius,'" Sierra said, tapping on her tablet. "Got it."

So her name was Sierra. Nice name for a nice-looking girl. I watched Sierra busily taking notes until Sanford's voice interrupted my thoughts.

"If we do hire you as waiters," Sanford said, "there'll be a dress code."

"That's no problem, sir," I said. "Joe and I own suits."

"Oh, not suits," Sanford said. "Togas."

"Togas?" I repeated.

"You mean those sheets the guys in ancient Rome used to wrap themselves up in?" Chet asked, wide-eyed.

I glanced sideways at Joe, who didn't look too thrilled either. Was this Sweet Sixteen really worth it? But when I turned to look at Sierra, I got my answer. You bet!

"I'm sure we can get togas," I said.

"Or some white tablecloths from our mom," Joe added.

Lindsay tapped her chin as she studied us one at a time. She pointed to me, then to Joe.

"Those two can be waiters," Lindsay said.

"Just me and Frank?" Joe asked, surprised. "What about Chet?"

Sanford didn't even look at Chet as he went on with the party details.

"The Sweet Sixteen will be held this Sunday night, being that the next day is a holiday," Sanford said. "That gives us a whole day on Saturday to prepare food, the decorations—"

"My outfits!" Lindsay cut in.

I could see Chet making a time-out sign with his hands. "Excuse me," he said. "But what about me? Aren't I going to work this party too?"

"Maybe," Lindsay said. She turned to Sierra. "Put that one on the B-list. We can always call him if we get desperate."

"B-list?" Chet muttered.

Sanford looked at Joe and me and said, "Well? Don't you want your job instructions?"

I glanced over at Chet, who looked like he'd just been kicked in the stomach.

"No, thank you, sir," I said, standing up. "It's either all of us or none of us."

Joe stared at me before jumping up from his seat too. "Yeah," he said. "Come on, Chet, let's go."

"Are you guys crazy?" Lindsay cried as the three of us headed for the door. "Do you realize how amazing this party will be? You never know who you might meet!"

"If the kids are anything like you," Joe mumbled, "that's what we're afraid of."

I wasn't sure whether Sierra or the Peytons had heard Joe, and I didn't want to find out. All I wanted to do was get out of that house ASAP!

"B-list," Chet kept repeating once we were outside. "Why do you think Lindsay put me on the B-list?"

"*B* for 'bodacious,' dude," Joe said, laughing. "That's you!"

Chet cracked a smile.

"Forget about Princess Lindsay, Chet," I said. "I heard Bay Academy kids can be snooty—but that one takes the cake."

"Wrong!" Chet declared. He pulled a squished iced pastry from his jacket pocket. "I took the cake—on our way out!"

"Oh, snap!" Joe laughed.

As we walked to my car, I had no trouble forgetting about Lindsay, but Sierra kept popping into my head. Then, as if Joe had read my mind . . .

"I saw you watching that Sierra, Frank," he said with a grin.

"You never miss a beat, do you?" I smirked.

Joe shrugged and said, "Just saying!"

Leaving the sprawling Peyton mansion behind us, we walked down the flagstone path toward the private parking lot. I could see my car in the distance right where I'd parked it. But before we could get to my secondhand fuel-efficient sedan, we had to pass a parking lot full of luxury SUVs and sports cars.

"Boats and cars," I sighed. "How many fancy toys can one family have?"

"Not enough if you're a Peyton," Chet said. "Which ride do you think is Empress Lindsay's?"

Joe pointed to a red sports convertible whose vanity plate read LUV2SHOP. "I'll take a wild guess and say that one!" he chuckled.

Chet whistled through his teeth as we went to check out the shiny car. The top was down, so we got a good look.

"Black leather seating," I observed as the three of us walked slowly around the car. "MP3 output . . ."

"Yeah, and I'll bet that's a heated steering wheel," Chet added.

"That's not all it has, you guys," Joe called.

Glancing up, I saw my brother staring at the car door. He didn't look impressed. Just dead serious.

"What's up?" I asked.

Without saying a word, Joe pointed to the door. I turned to see what he was pointing at. That's when my jaw practically hit the ground—because scratched across the gleaming car were the angry words:

2

BAD APPETITE

JOE

THE THREE OF US GAWKED AT THE DOOR
and the message. I had seen keyed cars before—
but never scratches as deep as this.

"Whoa," Frank said. "A keyed car has got to
be the worst kind of prank."

"Worse than a million hurled slushies," Chet agreed.

The word "slushies" made me remember the YouTube
video—and the clueless punks who starred in it.

"You guys," I said. "What if this was done by the same
slushie-slingers we saw in the video clip?"

Frank gave it a thought, then shook his head. "I don't
think so," he said.

"How come?" I asked.

"Because I think it was another Sweet Sixteen reject,"

Frank explained. "Who knows how many kids Lindsay dissed by putting on the B-list today?"

"And watch out," Chet joked. "When provoked, we B-listers can get pretty ugly."

I ran my finger along the deep scratches. Frank was probably right.

"It wasn't one of Lindsay's friends, because they're probably rich too," I thought out loud. "It probably *was* a reject like us."

"Hey, you guys weren't rejected from working that party," Chet reminded us. "You can still be fitted for your togas, you know."

"Thanks, but no thanks," Frank said. "Lindsay's Sweet Sixteen may be the party of the decade, but it's not worth the humiliation."

"And who needs all that fancy-schmancy food when you can get the most awesome burgers and fries at Chomp and Chew?" I added.

Chet's eyes lit up at the magic words. "Chomp and Chew, huh?" he asked with a smile. "Could that be a hint?"

Frank shook his head as he pointed to the scratches on the car door. "Wait a minute, you guys," he said. "What are we going to do about Lindsay's car?"

"What do you mean?" I asked.

"I mean, should we tell Lindsay about the scratches?" Frank asked. "She really ought to know."

I glanced back at the Peyton house. Sure, I felt bad for

Empress Lindsay and her trashed car. But the thought of facing her and her dad again practically made my skin crawl.

"Nah," I said. "She'll find out soon enough."

We took one last look at the scratches before walking away.

"What do you think Lindsay will do when she sees her keyed car?" Chet asked.

"Get Daddy to buy her a new one?" I said with a shrug.

The Chomp and Chew was only a fifteen-minute drive from the Peytons'. You couldn't miss the place, with its giant neon burger spinning on the roof. It may have been super tacky, but the burgers were tastier than filet mignon. . . . Not that I'd ever tasted filet mignon.

By the time we were cozy in the booth next to the window and under the TV, we had forgotten all about Lindsay and her keyed car. All we could think about were the burgers we were chomping and chewing: guacamole burger for me, Western burger for Frank, and the everything burger for Chet.

"Our favorite burgers and our favorite booth!" Chet said, popping a pickle chip into his mouth. "Are we lucky or what?"

My mouth was too stuffed to answer, so I gave Chet a nod. As my eyes began to drift up toward the TV, I spotted someone I knew from school. It was Tony, a Bayport High senior like Frank. But Tony wasn't happily chomping or chewing like us. He was crazy busy clearing dirty dishes and glasses from a nearby booth.

"There's Tony Riley," I whispered to Frank and Chet. "I didn't know he worked as a busboy here."

We watched as Tony picked up his tip. He looked at it, rolled his eyes, and murmured something under his breath.

"The guy definitely looks overworked," Frank whispered.

I felt bad for Tony and wanted to cheer him up. So I waved and called, "Yo, Tony! I'll bet free burgers come with the job, huh?"

Tony dropped his rag on the table and walked over to our booth.

"Who cares about that?" he said in a low voice. "After working in this place almost all day, the last thing I want is a Chomp and Chew burger."

"Wow," Chet said, shaking his head. "This place must really be a sweatshop for you to pass up a Chomp and Chew burger."

Tony snorted and said, "Working in a sweatshop would be a breeze compared to this place. A kid in the last booth just wrote his name on the table with ketchup!"

"What was his name?" I asked.

"Al," Tony replied.

"At least it's only two letters," Frank said.

"He wrote his full name, guys!" Tony sighed. "Alexander!"

"Bummer," I said. Maybe that sweatshop *was* a better deal.

"If you hate it that much, Tony," Frank said, lowering his voice, "why don't you just look for another job?"

"Part-time jobs aren't so easy to get, Frank," Tony explained.

"And I'm saving up for a new phone, so I can't quit now."

Frank nodded as if to say he got it.

"Frank and I can't even have fancy phones yet," I said. "But this is the next best thing."

"What is?" Tony asked.

"Glad you asked," I said, pulling out my tablet. "Tony, my man, when was the last time you saw a skateboarding squirrel?"

"Spare me, Joe," Frank groaned.

But Tony finally cracked a smile. "Squirrels on skateboards—no way!" He laughed. "Let me see that."

I was about to search for the clip when a voice shouted, "Yo, busboy! Why don't you start earning your minimum wage?"

Tony froze. So did we. Who'd said that?

Turning my head, I saw a bunch of guys in a nearby booth laughing it up. They were wearing polo shirts and khaki pants. One of the guys had on a Bay Academy varsity jacket.

"Bunch of jerks," Chet said. "Who do those guys think they are?"

"They're Bay Academy kids, that's who," Frank whispered. "No doubt they'll be going to Lindsay's Sweet Sixteen."

"Yeah," I scoffed. "But they won't be passing around barbecued hot wings and punch."

Looking at Tony, I could tell he was trying hard to keep his cool.

"No problem, guys," he called back. "I'll be there in a minute."

"A minute isn't good enough!" the guy with a maroon polo shirt and wavy blond hair boomed. "This table here is pretty messy."

His friends snickered as he picked up a half-full glass of chocolate shake and poured it all over the table!

Tony's face turned beet red, but he kept his mouth shut.

Not me . . .

"Hey, losers!" I shouted toward the booth. "Why don't you clean up your own mess?"

"Yeah, well, why don't you shut up?" the guy with the biggest mouth snapped.

"Game over," Frank muttered as he stood up.

He looked like he was about to go over to the Bay Academy booth, until we all saw someone in a police uniform heading up the aisle.

"Sweet," I said. "Somebody must have called the cops on those guys."

As detectives, Frank and I knew all the officers in Bayport. Sometimes we'd ask them for advice on a case we were working on. Sometimes they'd even ask us for advice, which was really cool.

Most of the officers were great guys—minus one named Officer Olaf. His beef with Frank and me was that we were always trying to do his job. Lucky for us, the cop at the Chomp and Chew was Officer Schroeder.

I expected Officer Schroeder to stop at the Bay Academy booth. Instead, he walked right past them, straight to us.

"Boys," he said with a nod. "The chief wants you to come to the station right away."

Frank and I traded confused looks.

"We've retired from investigating, Officer Schroeder," I said.

"It's not about a case, Joe," Officer Schroeder said. "It's about the gash on Lindsay Peyton's car."

"Oh!" Frank said with a nod. "Does the chief want to know what we saw?"

Officer Schroeder's mouth became a grim line. "No," he said. "The chief wants to know what you did."

MISINFORMED 3

FRANK

THIS DIDN'T LOOK GOOD.

"Excuse me, Officer Schroeder," I said. "Does the chief think that we keyed Lindsay's car?"

The officer heaved a sigh. I could tell he wasn't thrilled with the situation. All the cops had known us since we were little kids.

"You can ask all the questions you want at the station," he explained. "Come on, guys, pay your bill and let's go."

"Okay," Chet said. "But can we at least get our burgers to go?"

"Chet, just pay," I murmured.

Quickly and quietly we laid our money on the table before we left. By now all eyes in the Chomp and Chew were on us as we followed Officer Schroeder up the aisle.

I knew we weren't criminals, but I sure felt like one.

"Good luck, guys," Tony whispered as we walked past him. "Whatever this is all about."

"Thanks," I whispered back.

I could hear snickering as we passed the Bay Academy booth. I tried not to look at the creeps until one of them sneered, "Bad day, burger boys?"

Without even looking, I knew who it was—the idiot who'd tipped over the chocolate shake.

"Surprise, surprise," Joe said, loud enough for the whole booth to hear. "I thought they didn't allow animals in here."

"Will you quit it, Joe?" I muttered. "The last thing we need is more trouble."

Once outside, we followed Officer Schroeder to the squad car. He walked a good few feet ahead of us, giving us some privacy.

"I knew it," I murmured. "I knew we should have told Lindsay about her car."

"Frank, I just had a weird thought," Joe said quietly.

"What?" I asked.

"What if they dust the car for fingerprints?" Joe squeaked. "I ran my finger along the scratch—about three times."

"You think that's bad?" Chet said. "I snatched a pastry on the way out. What was I thinking?"

All I knew was that this was serious stuff.

"Look," I said. "When we get to the station, we'll just tell Chief Gomez the truth. He's known for being fair."

"Um . . . FYI," Chet said. "I heard Chief Gomez retired about a week ago. Some other officer at the station was just promoted to chief."

"Which one?" I asked.

"How should I know?" Chet said. "You're the detectives."

"Well, that explains it, then," I said. "This new chief, whoever he or she is, probably wants to be extra thorough. You know, cover all the bases."

"If you say so," Joe said. "I just hope covering all the bases doesn't mean fingerprints!"

We left my car in the Chomp and Chew parking lot, and Officer Schroeder drove us to the station. Joe and I were glad he didn't run the siren—the last thing we wanted was more attention.

The ride to the station was only fifteen minutes but felt like fifteen hours. When we arrived, Officer Schroeder led us to the receiving desk. I was almost anxious to see the chief and get this over with. If he or she was as fair as Chief Gomez, we'd be out of here in a matter of minutes.

"I've got the Hardy brothers and the Morton kid," Officer Schroeder said.

"Okay," the officer behind the desk said. "Chief Olaf said he'd see them right away."

Chief Olaf?

I stared at Joe, who looked about as sick as I felt. If the new chief of police was Officer Olaf, we did not have a chance!

"Yo, Frank," Joe whispered as we followed another officer down a long hallway.

"What?" I whispered back.

"Do you think they have wi-fi in the slammer?" Joe asked.

"Whatever," I mumbled.

The new chief of police, Olaf, was sitting behind his desk as we filed into his office. He looked up at us and immediately scowled.

"If you Hardys think you're off the hook because your father was a private investigator, well, think again!" he barked.

"We weren't planning on playing the dad card, Officer— I mean, Chief Olaf," Joe said.

"What exactly is this all about, Chief?" I asked carefully.

"Didn't Schroeder tell you?" Chief Olaf demanded. "Something nasty was scratched on the door of Lindsay Peyton's very expensive car."

"We know about that," Chet blurted.

"You bet you know," Chief Olaf said. "You boys were at the house at the time of the incident. Someone even saw you hanging around Lindsay's car in the parking lot."

Someone? I wondered who had gone to the police about us. Was it Sanford Peyton? Lindsay herself?

"We were at the house, Chief, that's true," I said. "But we were there to apply for a job, not to make trouble."

The chief leaned forward. "And this job would get you into one of the biggest parties in Bayport, right?"

"Lindsay's Sweet Sixteen," Joe said with a nod.

"Well, you didn't take the job, did you?" Chief Olaf asked. "In fact, you left the place pretty steamed, am I right, boys?"

"They called me B-list material!" Chet blurted. "How would you feel?"

I gave Chet a quick but subtle elbow jab. He had a habit of stuffing his mouth—and running it too.

"Well?" Chief Olaf asked, leaning back in his big leather chair. "So what's the story?"

"Chief, you know we're detectives," I said.

The chief raised an eyebrow. "Last I checked, your dad and I discussed that you should concentrate on other things."

"Okay, we *were* detectives," I said quickly.

"We solved crimes," Joe added. "We don't commit them."

"Then what about that guy?" the chief said, leaning over to point at Chet. "Mr. Peyton said he stole a pastry!"

"Rats!" Chet hissed.

I took a deep breath, trying to keep my cool. "Chief Olaf, we had nothing to do with Lindsay's car being keyed," I said. "We can even prove it if you just give us a little time."

"I think this prank had something to do with another one that happened yesterday," Joe said.

"Show him the video, Joe!" Chet urged.

But the second Joe took out his tablet, the chief held up his hand as if to say, *Stop*.

"This is nothing new," Chief Olaf said. "Those pranks have been going on around Bayport for weeks."

"Weeks?" I said, surprised.

22

"Then you'll definitely want to look at this, Chief," Joe said, holding out his tablet.

"Why? So I can watch Katy Perry, or whoever it is you kids like these days?" Chief Olaf growled. "And as for you guys working on another case—give me a break. My best officers can't even catch those punks."

"Those punks?" Chet said hopefully. "As in . . . someone else?"

"So you believe us when we say we didn't key Lindsay's car?" I asked slowly.

Chief Olaf narrowed his steely blue eyes straight at us. "Let's just say I'm letting you go with a warning," he said.

I could hear Chet sigh with relief. I, too, was relieved. We were finally off the hook . . . or were we?

"But just remember that I'm keeping my eyes on all you kids," Chief Olaf said sternly. "Even you so-called detectives."

So-called detectives? Ouch! Technically, we weren't supposed to do any more investigating after our last adventure (if you call having a crime gang coming after you an adventure), but since we helped put away the Red Arrow, Dad and Chief Olaf made us a deal that if we checked in and made sure to follow a few guidelines, we could still catch a few bad guys every now and then. Most important, we wouldn't be sent to the notorious J'Adoube School for Behavior Modification. And it looks like we might be catching bad guys sooner than expected.

When the chief opened the door, we couldn't get out fast enough. We walked quickly up the hallway, not looking back.

"So-called detectives," Joe scoffed. "He's just jealous because we're good at doing his job."

"Joe, keep it down!" I warned. "The last thing we need is more trouble with the new chief."

"But Olaf practically said we're clean!" Joe insisted.

"Let's just get out of here," I said as we stepped into the waiting area.

"Are you sure you want to leave?" Chet asked.

"Yeah, why?" I asked. I followed Chet's gaze to the long wooden bench against the wall. Sitting on it were an elderly woman, a middle-aged man, and . . . Sierra?

My eyes widened as the pretty, dark-haired girl stood up and smiled in our direction. It was Sierra, all right. But what was she doing at the station, of all places?

That's when it suddenly clicked—and when my admiration turned into anger. The person who'd gone to the cops about us wasn't Sanford Peyton or Lindsay.

It was Sierra!

CLUED IN 4

JOE

I DIDN'T HAVE TO READ FRANK'S MIND TO KNOW he was thinking the same as me—had Sierra told on us to the cops?

"So you're the informant," Frank said as Sierra walked toward us.

"Informant?" she asked with a smile.

"Let me put it in plain English," I said. "Did you come to the cops to tell them we keyed Lindsay's car?"

Sierra's smile turned into a frown. "I saw what happened, and it's such a bummer," she said. "Lindsay adores that car."

"I believe that," Frank said. "So why didn't the chief look totally convinced that we didn't key it?"

"I believe you," Sierra said, tilting her head and looking

all flirty. "You're not gladiator material—or vandal material, for that matter."

"Did you tell that to Mr. Peyton?" I asked.

"How could I?" Sierra said, her eyes wide. "He was already on the phone with the chief."

Okay. That explained who'd called the cops, but it didn't explain what Sierra was doing at the police station.

"So, do you come here often?" I joked. "Must be the free coffee and doughnuts."

"I happen to drink tea," Sierra said. "And I'm here because Mr. Peyton wanted me to make sure the Sweet Sixteen had the police presence he requested."

Frank looked relieved to find out that Sierra wasn't the snitch. "If you ask me," he said, "that party is going to need the whole force."

"What do you mean?" Sierra asked.

"With all those kids from Bay Academy," Frank said, "the place will be oozing with bling, fancy watches, and state-of-the-art phones."

"Hey, no fair," Sierra said, faking at being insulted. "I go to Bay Academy."

I could practically hear Frank gulp.

"Awkward," Chet said under his breath.

"Um—you do?" Frank asked, turning red. "I had no idea. You don't seem like . . . I mean—"

"It's okay," Sierra laughed. "Oh, and FYI, I wasn't invited to Lindsay's Sweet Sixteen either."

"You weren't invited?" I asked, surprised. "And you don't mind doing all this grunt work for the Peytons?"

Sierra shook her head.

"I'm interning for the head event planner of the party. It's what I want to do after I graduate college, so it's really good experience," she explained. "Although walking Lindsay's yappy little dog was definitely not in my job description."

Frank laughed, a little too loudly. He blushed when the officer behind the desk cleared her throat.

"So you go to Bay Academy," Frank said, lowering his voice. "I guess that means you don't date Bayport High guys."

Whoa. Frank wasn't exactly smooth when it came to girls, so for him to make a move, he'd have to be pretty serious.

Chet and I turned to Sierra for her reaction. She flashed Frank a sly smile before pulling out a pen. Then she picked up Frank's hand and wrote her name and number on his palm.

"Why don't you call me and find out?" Sierra said with a grin.

Man, I thought. *If Frank wasn't already crushing on this girl, I might!*

Chet glanced at Frank's scribbled-on palm. "If you do go out with Frank . . . Sierra Mitchell," he said, "you won't be sorry, that's for sure."

"What do you mean?" Sierra asked.

"Yeah," Frank demanded. "What do you mean?"

"Because Frank is the best detective in Bayport, that's what I mean," Chet said. "Other than his brother, Joe, here, of course."

"We're a team," I added quickly.

Sierra tilted her head to study Frank, then me. "Detectives?" she asked. "Seriously?"

"Not only that," Chet went on, "Frank and Joe are going to find out who keyed Lindsay's car if they have to turn this jerkwater town upside down!"

"We are?" Frank cried.

It was news to me, too, but the most surprised seemed to be Sierra. Her eyes lit up like headlights as she said, "You are?"

Frank stared back at Sierra. Then he smiled and said, "Um . . . yeah, sure."

"I guess that means we're on the case," I said.

"Okay, kids," the officer behind the desk snapped. "This isn't a bowling alley—time to socialize somewhere else."

"We were just leaving, Officer," Frank said.

"And I'm here on business," Sierra told her.

Frank gave Sierra a little wave before we headed out of the station. We had to walk along the road back to Frank's car, still parked at the Chomp and Chew. It was a long walk, but we were just happy to get out of the station. As for Frank, he looked just plain happy!

"Who knew getting arrested would be a great way to meet girls, huh, Frank?" I teased.

"We weren't arrested, we were just warned," Frank said. "And all Sierra did was give me her number, so the ball is in my court."

"Yeah, right," Chet chuckled. "Just make sure you don't wash that hand, dude."

We were having a good laugh when I heard the fired-up engine of a speeding car. I turned just in time to see a shiny black Benz barreling down the road. Frank, Chet, and I stopped to watch the car as it came our way. A car window came down and . . . *CLUNK!!* An empty soda can was hurled out the window, barely missing Chet!

"Hey!" Chet yelled.

The Benz kept going, so fast I didn't see who was inside. But I could hear them laughing—and it sounded exactly like the guys at the Chomp and Chew!

"Jerks!" I called after the car.

"Hey, Chet," Frank asked, "are you okay, buddy?"

"Yeah, sure," Chet said with a nod. "Who do you think those guys were?"

"It had to be those Bay Academy losers," I said angrily. "The ones who were giving Tony a hard time at the Chomp and Chew."

Chet kicked the can away. "What's with those Bay Academy kids, anyway?" he wondered aloud as we continued walking up the road. "I mean, why are they being such morons?"

"Come on, Chet," Frank said. "Not all Bay Academy kids are bad news."

I raised an eyebrow at my brother.

"Hmm," I teased. "And does her name happen to be Sierra?"

Frank gave me a little push. "Okay, you guys," he said. "Now that we're on the case, we've got to get serious about Lindsay's car. Who do you think could have done it?"

"I still think the punks who slushied Lonny are the punks who keyed the car." I patted the pocket holding my tablet. "And if that stunt goes viral—we'll know for sure!"

"No games at the dinner table, Joe," Mom said as she placed a platter of lasagna inches away from me. "You know the rules."

I looked up from my tablet and said, "But it's not a game, Mom. I'm looking to see if any more pranks went viral."

"We're working on a new case," Frank explained. "Somebody scratched up Lindsay Peyton's car. We want to find out who did it."

Dad stopped piling lasagna on his plate. "Are you sure that's a good idea, guys?" he asked. "After what happened today with Chief Olaf?"

We had already told Dad about being called to the police station. He wanted to call Chief Olaf, but we begged him not to play the dad card.

"Dad, we're not going to stop working on cases just because the chief thinks we're detective wannabes," I said.

Dad nodded as if he understood. Fenton Hardy had

worked as a detective for decades. He did some occasional consulting still, but was focused on writing full-time.

"Plus, the faster we find the real culprits," Frank said, "the faster the chief will stop blaming innocent kids around Bayport—"

"Like us," I cut in.

"Okay," Dad said, taking a helping of salad. "Then go for it."

Mom cleared her throat to get my attention.

"You may have won Dad's argument, Joe," Mom said, narrowing her eyes at my tablet. "But you didn't win mine."

"Okay, okay," I said, putting it away.

Our mom, Laura Hardy, was a star real estate agent in Bayport. She could convince anyone to buy a home—or put away their tablets at dinner.

I was just about to pile some lasagna on my own plate when I saw Frank sniffing the air.

"What's that smell?" Frank asked, wiggling his nose.

"Grated cheese?" I guessed.

"No," Dad groaned. "It's your aunt Trudy burning those smelly scented candles again."

"But Aunt Trudy lives in the apartment above the garage," I said. "How can we smell them all the way over here?"

"Because that's how potent they are," Dad said. "If you ask me, they smell more like rotten eggs than spring rain and patchouli."

"Eggs—that reminds me," Mom said. "Someone at work told me there was a prank at the library last night."

Prank? My ears perked up like a dog hearing a whistle.

"What kind of prank, Mom?" I asked.

"Something about someone throwing eggs down the book drop," Mom said, shaking her head. "A half dozen books were totally ruined."

Frank shot me a look across the table. Another prank in Bayport? Now I really wanted to check out YouTube to see if it had gone viral. I had a feeling Frank did too.

The two of us practically inhaled our lasagna. As soon as we were excused, we raced up the stairs to my room. We sat down on the floor—but not before I tossed aside a bunch of dirty socks, a hoodie, some notebooks, and a half-eaten banana.

"Sometimes I can't believe we have the same DNA." Frank sighed. "When are you going to clean up this place?"

"I just did," I said. "You should have seen it before."

"How are we going to find it?" Frank asked. "There are millions of videos on YouTube."

"We could search 'egg pranks,'" I said as I turned on the tablet. But before I typed in a search, I had another idea. "Or . . . we could find the user name for the slushie video."

"What good would that do?" Frank asked.

"We can do a search of the user name and see if he or she posted the egg prank," I explained.

"Go for it," Frank said.

It didn't take me long to find the infamous slushie-slinger clip. It was posted by some guy who called himself "slickbro13."

"Slickbro13, slickbro13," I repeated. "What do you think the number thirteen stands for?"

"Bad luck?" Frank guessed.

"It was definitely bad luck for Lonny," I said as I searched for more slickbro13 clips.

It didn't take long to find what we were looking for. Not only did we find a clip of the egg drop crime at the library, we found other videos of window smashings, Dumpster tippings—even more slushy slingings at different fast-food places. And all of them posted by slickbro13.

"This must be the vandalism Chief Olaf was talking about," Frank said. "The ones that happened over the last few weeks."

I checked to see the dates on some of the clips. They had been posted during that time.

"Who are the kids in the videos?" I wondered.

To get a better look, we switched over to my computer. There I was able to enlarge the videos, even pause them at certain points. It helped, but not enough.

"The vandals are wearing dark bandannas over their faces," Frank pointed out. "The videos were also shot at night, which makes it extra hard to identify them."

"Why do you think they posted their pranks, Frank?" I asked. "On YouTube of all places, for everybody to see?"

Frank shrugged and said, "Probably to show off. Or maybe as a message to the cops to catch them if they can."

The cops made me think of Lindsay's vandalized car. After a quick search, I found a video of that prank too. But since all we could see was the vandal's hand scratching the car, it was even harder to make out.

"Great," Frank complained.

I reran the video, carefully watching the hand as it used a key to scratch out the words RICH WITCH.

For some reason this prank had been pulled during the day, not night. Not only could I see the color of Lindsay's car, I could make out the color of the vandal's sleeve—dark green with gold trim. Colors I had seen many times before.

"Frank," I said, "that sleeve has our school colors on it!"

Frank leaned forward for a better look. He turned to me and said, "That's our school varsity jacket. I'm almost sure of it."

"That's what I thought," I said. "We may not know who those viral vandals are, but we know where they are."

"Yeah," Frank said with a deep frown. "Our school!"

FOUND 5

FRANK

AS I DROVE TO SCHOOL THE NEXT MORNing, I kept my eyes on the road and my mind on the case. We now knew that one of the viral vandals went to Bayport High. It didn't tell us who the culprit was, but it was a pretty good start.

"Here's the plan," I said, stopping at the light. "We're going to check out every kid in our classes for clues."

"Every kid?" Joe said from the passenger seat. "What do we look for?"

"Varsity jackets, for one," I said. "Then there are those dark bandannas."

"As if the vandals are going to wear bandannas over their faces at school." Joe rolled his eyes.

"Just keep your eyes peeled, that's all I'm saying," I said as I drove around the corner. Bayport High School was halfway up the street. As I pulled up to the school, I noticed a bunch of teachers and kids crowded around the basketball court.

"A game so early?" I wondered out loud.

"Maybe it's practice," Joe figured.

I parked in the student parking lot. As Joe and I made our way to the court, I could see Principal Vega. He was shaking his head slowly as he spoke to the big guy in a beige suit. At first I thought it was Mr. Sweeney, the history teacher, but as we got closer, my stomach did a triple flip.

"Principal Vega is talking to Chief Olaf," I groaned under my breath.

"Do you think the chief is here about us?" Joe asked.

"Doubtful," I said. "Maybe Chief Olaf figured out that the vandals go to our school."

Joe and I joined Chet and his sister Iola near the basketball court. Iola Morton was the same age as Joe and just as fearless. She didn't look much like Chet, but their appetites for burgers were practically identical.

"What's up?" I asked.

"Check it out," Chet said.

I looked to see where Chet was pointing. Sprayed across the basketball court in red paint was the word "Scaredevils."

"Scaredevils," Joe read out loud. "Sounds like some kind of gang."

"Yeah," I said, staring at the tag. "A gang of viral vandals."

"Chet told me about the slushie clip," Iola asked. "Were there more?"

"We found a YouTube video of the car keying," Joe explained. "The vandals might be Bayport High students."

"No way," Chet said.

"Does Principal Vega know?" Iola asked.

"He will as soon as we tell him," I said. "Chief Olaf ought to know what we found out too."

"You're going to deal with Olaf again?" Chet groaned. "Good luck."

"Thanks, dude," Joe said. "Something tells me we're going to need it."

Joe and I squeezed through a crowd of kids to get to the principal and Chief Olaf. The chief frowned when he saw us.

"Principal Vega," I said, "Joe and I might have some information about this tag."

"And it's not about us!" Joe said, looking straight at Chief Olaf.

Principal Vega was new to Bayport High, but he knew we had done detective work in the past.

"All right, then, boys," Principal Vega said. "What do you know?"

The other students crowded closer to hear. Just in case some of them might be Scaredevils, I kept my voice low.

"We think some of the vandals go to Bayport High," I said.

Joe nodded at the tag on the basketball court. "Like that Scaredevils gang," he said.

"Gang?" Principal Vega shook his head and said, "That's highly unlikely."

"Why?" Joe asked.

"I may have been here only a few weeks," Principal Vega said, "but I know that Bayport High School has no gang activity—and never will, if I can help it."

"But—" I started to say.

"Don't you have a class to go to, Hardys?" Chief Olaf cut in.

"Don't you want to know what we found out?" Joe asked.

"Sir," I quickly added.

Chief Olaf opened his mouth to say something, but Principal Vega piped up.

"Thank you, Frank, Joe," the principal said. "But the chief and I have got this covered."

Joe and I sulked away from the basketball court. I wasn't surprised that Chief Olaf didn't believe us, but Principal Vega wouldn't even hear us out!

"Well, that was a total waste," I grumbled.

"I'll bet some Scaredevils were nearby having a good laugh too," Joe said.

We were about to walk back to Chet and Iola when Joe suddenly said, "Frank—look over there."

"What?" I asked.

Joe nodded toward the street. "That black Benz outside the school," he said. "Didn't we see that car some-where?"

I turned to look at the car. It did look familiar, and right away I knew why. . . .

"That's the car that soda can was thrown from," I said. "The one that almost hit Chet."

I recognized the pugnacious face staring out of the car window too. It was the Bay Academy guy from the Chomp and Chew.

"What's he doing at our school?" I asked. "That's what I'd like to know."

"Seeing how the other half lives?" Joe scoffed.

The driver glared at me, then at Joe. He then grabbed the wheel and drove away, tires squealing.

We hurried to the curb to watch the car take off.

"Why would a Bay Academy kid care what was going on at our school?" I asked.

"Unless he had something to do with the tag on the basketball court," Joe said. "And the other pranks around Bayport."

"Too bad we don't know his name," I said.

"We might know more than you think," Joe said. "I caught the guy's vanity plate as he took off. He goes by—are you ready? Awesome Dude!"

"Awesome Dude?" I said. "Give me a break."

We still didn't know the driver's real name. But his vanity plate was a start.

Throughout the day, Joe and I gave ourselves the same assignment: to ask questions about the viral videos and the mysterious "Awesome Dude" in the black car.

Joe and I weren't in the same classes, but most of the kids we questioned didn't have a clue about the videos or the vanity plate. Some knew a couple of "awesome dudes," but they didn't drive expensive black cars. After school Joe was happy to check out his tablet for more viral videos. It didn't take long for him to find what he was looking for.

"Ta-daa!" Joe sang. He held up the viewing device triumphantly. "Slickbro13's clip of the basketball court prank."

This clip showed some punk waving a spray paint can as he tagged our basketball court. His back was to the camera, making his face unidentifiable.

"First Awesome Dude, now slickbro13," I said. "How can we find out who he is?"

Joe shrugged. "We can contact YouTube," he said. "Maybe they'll give us slickbro13's real name."

"Not a chance," I said. "No company would give that information out so easily—especially one as big as YouTube. They probably wouldn't even know."

"Maybe we'll have more luck with Dad," Joe said, pocketing the tablet. "It pays to have a private investigator in the family, even if he is supposed to be retired."

The word "retired" wasn't in Fenton Hardy's vocabulary. Even though he was supposed to be writing a book about the history of law enforcement, occasionally he went back to doing what he did best—fighting crime!

We ended up walking to Dad's office downtown. Even though he'd retired, he kept it for writing purposes. Sometimes (well, a lot of the time) the house isn't exactly quiet.

"Hi, guys," Dad said when he saw us.

"Hi, Dad," Joe said, plopping down on the cushy leather sofa. "What's up?"

"You tell me," Dad said. "How was school today?"

"Not great," I replied. "Some creeps spray painted a gang tag on our basketball court."

"Vandals again?" Dad said. "Do you have any leads?"

I nodded and said, "Some suspicious-looking kid was hanging out in front of the school this morning. He drove off before we could find out more."

"But I caught his vanity plate, Dad," Joe said proudly. "It's Awesome Dude!"

"Awesome?" Dad asked with a smirk. "Are you sure it wasn't Awful?"

"What we need now is his real name," I said. "That's where you come in."

"Me?" Dad asked, raising a brow.

"Could you please do a search and tell us who this Awesome Dude is, Dad?" Joe asked, jumping off the sofa. "I'm sure you private-eye guys have ways of finding out that stuff."

Dad immediately shook his head. "Sorry," he said. "But no can do."

"Why not?" Joe asked.

"Because license plates are federally protected information," Dad explained. "I never use those tracking methods unless it's an absolute emergency or I have a reason to."

"But it is an emergency, Dad," I said.

I was just about to explain why when another detective, Felix Cruz, strolled into the office.

"Fenton, old man!" Felix boomed. "I hear you're writing your memoirs."

"Trying to," Dad said with a grin.

"Well, don't forget to mention me!" Felix said, winking at Joe and me.

"You bet, Felix," Dad said. "You remember my boys, Frank and Joe?"

"Sure I do," Felix declared. He reached into his pocket and pulled out his phone. "Let me show you some recent pictures of my kids, Fenton. You won't believe how big they've gotten."

Dad smiled politely as Felix flashed pictures of his five kids.

"I have a feeling this is going to take a while," I whispered to Joe. "We'd better go."

We left just as Felix was describing his son's birthday party at Charlie Cheese. Once in the hall, Joe turned to me. "Why did Dad give us such a hard time about the vanity plate?" he asked.

"He may be retired, but when it comes to detective work, he still goes by the book," I said.

"Some things never change." I sighed.

Suddenly we heard a voice hiss, "Psst. Psst."

Turning, I saw a woman with short, curly black hair waving us into her office. It was Connie Fleishman, another detective. Joe and I smiled. Out of all of Dad's coworkers, Connie was the coolest—always showing off her state-of-the-art spy gadgets and gizmos.

"Hi, Connie!" I said.

"What's up?" Joe asked.

"I've got something for you guys," Connie said. She grinned as she held up something that looked like an earbud for an MP3 player. "Guess what this is? Take a wild guess."

"Um . . . can I listen to music with it?" Joe guessed.

"It does a lot more than that, Joey," Connie said. "Pop this in your ear and you'll be able to hear conversations up to one hundred feet away. Even whispers."

"Cool," I said.

"Way cool!" Joe said.

"Here. Consider it a gift," Connie said, slipping it into Joe's hand. "So what are you guys doing here today? Visiting the old man?"

"Sort of," I said. "We were hoping Dad would give us the name of the owner of a vanity plate we saw."

"But according to Dad, that information is top secret," Joe added.

Connie snorted and flapped her hand. "Your dad's retired," she said. "I'm the big cheese here now."

Connie waved us to her computer. After about five minutes

of searching files, she was able to give us the full name of Awesome Dude.

"Colin Sylvester," Connie reported. "Name ring a bell?"

"I think so," I said slowly. "Don't his parents own a line of cruise ships or something?"

"Whatever they do, they're superrich," Joe said. "I think they have a house by the bay that makes the Peytons' look like a shack."

"Is there anything else you want me to look up while I'm here?" Connie asked.

I thought about the YouTube clip and slickbro13, but shook my head. "You've done plenty for us already, Connie," I said. "And if Dad finds out—"

"Tell him whatever you want," Connie said with a grin. "If he doesn't like it, I'll probably read about it in that book of his."

We left Dad's office building with the best clue we'd gotten all day—the name of the guy in the black Benz.

"Now we know that it was Colin Sylvester outside our school today," I said when we were halfway home. "But we still don't know why he was there."

Joe shrugged and said, "Maybe it's no big deal. Maybe he saw the commotion and stopped his car to be nosy."

"With that look he gave us?" I said, remembering the icy glare. "I don't think so."

We were walking up Foley Street when Joe's tablet beeped.

"What was that?" I asked.

"I got a text or an e-mail," he said, pulling it out.

"That thing gets e-mails too?" I said, impressed. "It really can do everything."

Joe stopped to check out the e-mail. He wrinkled his brow and said, "I don't recognize the sender. There's an attachment, too."

"Then delete!" I declared. "Never open an attachment you don't recognize."

"Too late," Joe said. "I already did."

I peered over Joe's shoulder as a video appeared on the small screen. As he and I watched the clip, our eyes popped wide open. It showed some guy hurling a rock through the window of Bayport's only flower shop. His back was to the camera as he jumped up and down, cheering.

"Another Scaredevil," I said through gritted teeth. "But why was it sent to you? That's what I want to know."

"Yeah, me too," Joe said. "And how did those lowlifes get my e-mail?"

Joe was about to replay the clip when I heard what sounded like heavy footsteps behind us. Spinning around, I saw two tall, beefy guys coming our way. I blinked hard when I saw what they wore: steel breastplates, leather sandals—and heavy, glistening swords!

"Um . . . Frank?" Joe said when he saw them too. "Who are those guys?"

"I don't know," I said. "All I do know is that they're armed—and dangerous."

INVITE ONLY 6

JOE

FRANK AND I STOOD FROZEN LIKE STATUES. The armored guys' eyes were on us as they came closer and closer. My own eyes stayed fixed on those swords!

"Either we're in a time warp," I murmured, "or I'm seeing ancient warriors."

"In case they attack," Frank said out of the corner of his mouth, "do we fight them off?"

"With what?" I whispered. "Our backpacks?"

The steel-plated giants came within inches of Frank and me. Before I could ask what they wanted, they made a sharp right turn. We watched as they headed straight up the front walkway of a large Colonial-style home.

"Who are those guys?" Frank asked.

One warrior rang the doorbell with the handle of his sword. While the two stood facing the door, Frank and I inched closer to the house and hid behind a shrub. We peeked out and watched as a woman wearing a white uniform opened the door.

"Hello, ma'am," one warrior said. "Is Stacy Chung here?"

The woman looked super nervous as she stepped away. In a matter of seconds a girl of about sixteen came to the door.

"Does she go to our school?" Frank whispered.

"I don't think so," I whispered back.

We watched as the other warrior held up what looked like a large square envelope. "Stacy Chung, lend us your ears!" he boomed. "By orders of the royal empire, you are hereby invited to the Sweet Sixteen of Empress Lindsay Peyton!"

The two then beat their chests and declared, "Veni, vidi, Versace!"

Stacy stood with her mouth open. Then, without warning, she let out an earsplitting shriek.

"Lindsay Peyton's Sweet Sixteen—no way!" Stacy screamed happily, jumping up and down. "No way! No way!"

I leaned over to Frank and said, "I get it. Those guys are the gladiators Lindsay was talking about at our interview."

"Yeah, but why is she getting an invitation today?" Frank said. "The party is this weekend."

We ducked behind the tree trunk as the gladiators

stomped by. I could hear one of them saying, "Was she the last on the B-list?"

"Yeah." The other one sighed. "Let's ditch these tin cans and get some pizza."

Stacy was still shrieking as the gladiators walked up the street.

"B-list," Frank scoffed, shaking his head. "No wonder her invitation's late."

"Let's go," I said. "Before Stacy detonates my eardrums."

"Not yet, Joe," Frank said. "If Stacy goes to Bay Academy, she might have some info on Colin."

Frank slipped out from behind the tree. I raced to catch up with him as he approached the house.

"Um—Stacy?" Frank called as she began to shut the door. "Can we ask you something?"

Stacy was still smiling from ear to ear as she said, "I think I've seen you guys around."

"I'm Frank Hardy, and this is my brother, Joe," Frank said. "You go to Bay Academy, right?"

"Right," Stacy said. She wrinkled her nose impatiently. "Um . . . is that all you want to know? I've got to text my friends and tell them the awesome news."

"Real quick," Frank promised. "Do you know a guy at your school named Colin Sylvester?"

Stacy rolled her eyes. "Unfortunately," she groaned, before holding up the invitation. "He won't be going to this party—that's for sure."

"How come?" I asked.

"Du-uh!" Stacy said. "Everybody knows Lindsay can't stand Colin."

"Why doesn't she like him?" Frank asked.

"It's complicated," Stacy said. "Look, I can't hang around and talk right now. I've got a gazillion things to do!"

"But—" Frank started to say.

"I've got to call Elise, Lily, and Beth, make a hair appointment, shop for a new dress and shoes. . . ."

Stacy's voice trailed off as she shut the door in our faces. We stood staring at the door before Frank said, "So Lindsay can't stand Colin."

"Can you blame her?" I said, walking away from the door. "Now can we forget about Colin for a minute and try to figure something out?"

"Like what?" Frank asked.

I turned to my brother and said, "Like—how did the Scaredevils get my e-mail address?"

"See?" I said, holding out my tablet. "More and more videos are going viral, and they're coming straight to me."

Frank, Chet, Iola, and I were holding court in our usual favorite booth at the Chomp and Chew. But no one was looking out the window or at the game on the TV. We were too busy checking out the latest viral video starring the Scaredevils. This one showed the same bunch of bandanna-sporting thugs setting a Dumpster on fire.

"That's enough to make anyone's skin crawl," Chet declared. His eyes then darted around the Chomp and Chew, busy with the dinner crowd. "Should we even be watching these videos out in the open like this?"

"Why not?" Iola asked.

"What if the Scaredevils are here?" Chet whispered. "They could like burgers too, you know."

Frank and I glanced around. The booths and tables were packed, probably because of the free dessert special they had that night.

"Doubtful," Frank said. "The Scaredevils strike mostly at night."

"Yeah, they're too busy being evil to stop for hot fudge sundaes," I scoffed.

"Speaking of," Chet said. "Where's our food? I'm starving."

"Eat a pickle chip," Iola said, pushing a dish of pickles and olives toward her brother. She then turned to Frank and me. "If the Scaredevils are a gang, how will you catch them? There could be dozens of members running around Bayport!"

"Every gang has a ringleader," Frank explained. "If we get him, we get the whole gang."

I was about to grab a pickle myself when my tablet began beeping. "Here we go again," I sighed.

"Is it from slickbro13?" Frank asked.

I glanced down at the user name. "Who else?" I said. "But this time he sent me a little message."

"What does it say?" Iola asked.

"Special delivery," I read out loud.

Everyone huddled around my tablet as I opened the attachment. The latest video was different from the others. Instead of showing vandalism, it showed two Scaredevils rolling on the ground in a fight. I turned up the volume to hear voices in the background, cheering them on.

"Why do you think they sent me a fight video?" I asked.

"Could be a warning," Chet said. "That next they're coming after you and Frank!"

"Thanks, pal," Frank said.

Chet shrugged and said, "Just saying."

But as I watched the fight clip, something about one of the guys looked familiar.

"I know this sounds crazy," I said. "But I think I know one of those guys."

"But you can't see their faces," Iola said, squinting to get a better look. "Can you?"

"It's not his face," I said, studying the video. "It's those long, skinny legs—"

"Okay, who gets the chunky chili burger with the sweet potato fries?" a voice asked, interrupting my thoughts.

I looked up to see a waiter holding a tray filled with our long-awaited burgers.

"Sweet potato fries, baby!" Chet said, hungrily rubbing his hands together. "Bring it!"

The last thing I wanted was pizza burger sauce all over my tablet. But just as I was about to put it away, Frank gave me a kick under the table.

"What?" I asked.

"Tony Riley's here," Frank said.

"So?" I said. "He works here."

Frank shook his head. "He's not bussing tables," he said. "He's sitting at that booth over there."

I followed Frank's gaze. Sure enough, Tony was in the house—sharing a booth with a cute red-haired girl. Tony was smiling coolly at her as he stretched his lanky leg into the aisle.

"I know her," Iola said as she shook a clogged ketchup bottle upside down. "That's Carolyn Meyer from school. She's in my gym class."

"Looks like Tony's on a date," I said. "It's probably his night off."

Frank furrowed his brow as if he didn't get it. "Why would Tony spend his night off in a place he hated?" he asked.

"Unless the guy quit," Chet said through a full mouth.

"Yeah, but he said he needed the money," Frank said. "To buy that phone he wanted."

"For a guy with no money, he sure ordered a ton of food," Iola pointed out.

"And if I'm not mistaken," Chet said, glancing over his shoulder, "that's the lobster burger Tony's eating—the most expensive thing on the menu."

Frank and I traded grins. If anyone was an authority on the Chomp and Chew menu, it was Chet.

"So the guy could have saved up," I said, glancing back at Tony. It was then that I noticed something other than his date and lobster burger.

Tony had what looked like a deep scratch under his left eye. When I quietly pointed it out, Chet said, "Tony works in a restaurant. Maybe it was some kind of kitchen accident."

"That," I said, "or some kind of fight."

"Tony in a fight?" Iola said unbelievingly. "He's so nice one of the teachers calls him Gentleman Riley."

Tony was a nice guy. Even if somebody did beat on him, he probably wouldn't fight back.

"I guess you're right," I decided.

I was about to turn away from Tony when I spotted his jacket hanging from a hook over his booth. Sticking out of a pocket was something dark blue with some kind of white paisley design.

"Whoa!" I gasped, realizing what it was.

It was a bandanna—a dark-blue bandanna!

7

SECRETS

FRANK

THIS TIME JOE KICKED ME UNDER THE table. I stared at my brother as if to say, *What?*

"Tony's jean jacket is hanging next to his booth," Joe said.

"And?" I asked.

"And take a look at what's sticking out of the pocket," he whispered.

I glanced over to Tony's booth and his jacket. Some kind of dark blue material with a white design was sticking out.

"Rhymes with . . . banana?" Joe hinted.

"Bandanna!" I said. "Tony's got a dark-blue bandanna in his pocket."

"You're kidding me, right?" Iola said, stretching her neck to see.

54

"It's a blue bandanna, all right," Chet confirmed. "Good catch, Joe."

"Thanks," Joe said. "But you know what this means, don't you?"

"Hard to believe," I said. "Tony Riley, a Scaredevil?"

Joe leaned forward, lowered his voice, and said, "No wonder the fighter in the video looked familiar. He had the same long, skinny legs as Tony's."

"So that was Tony fighting?" Iola said, scrunching up her nose. "The guy doesn't even arm wrestle in the school lunchroom for fun!"

Trying not to look obvious, I watched Tony eating his lobster burger. Sure, the scratch and the bandanna made him look guilty. But I wasn't going to accuse the guy until we got more facts. At least, that's the way Dad taught us.

"We've got to go over to Tony and ask him a bunch of questions," I told Joe. "Before he finishes his food and leaves the place."

"Okay," Joe said.

But Chet shook his head and said, "Nuh-uh. Not okay."

"Why not?" I asked.

"Because Tony is out with Carolyn," Chet explained. "And the last thing he'll want to do is answer questions in front of her."

"Especially since Carolyn Meyer is the ultimate gossip girl," Iola said. "No one talks in front of her unless they're totally clueless."

My shoulders slumped as I stared at the Mortons. Since when were they such drags?

"You guys," I complained. "If Tony is in the Scaredevils, he can lead us straight to the ringleader—whoever he is."

"Frank is right," Joe said. "We have to get him to spill."

"Any suggestions?" I asked Chet and Iola.

"Nope," Chet said, going back to his burger. But Iola flashed a smile and said, "I know what to do."

"What?" Joe asked.

"I'm going to tell Carolyn I just found something out that will make her teeth curl," Iola whispered.

"You mean you're going to lure her away with gossip?" Chet said. "As if any girl would leave a date to dish with another girl."

"This girl would," Iola said as she squeezed past me out of the booth. "Watch and learn."

The three of us did watch as Iola headed to Tony and Carolyn's booth. I had a feeling she was speaking extra loud so we could all hear.

"Carolyn, you're not going to believe the dirt I just dug up on Deanna DaCosta," Iola said.

"The captain of the girls' basketball team?" Carolyn gasped excitedly. "What are you waiting for? Spill!"

"Tony doesn't want to hear this," Iola said, smiling at Tony. "Come on, Carolyn. I'll tell you the whole story in the restroom."

"I'm there," Carolyn said, already halfway out of the booth. "I'll be right back, Tony."

"Yeah, sure," Tony said. He barely looked up from his lobster burger as Carolyn followed Iola up the aisle to the back.

"I can see who has the brains in the family!" Joe teased Chet.

"But I have the good looks!" Chet joked.

"Yeah, right," I said, smirking. "Joe, let's go over to Tony's table and see what we can get."

"What about me?" Chet asked.

"Stay here and make sure nobody eats our burgers," I said.

"Just let 'em try!" Chet chuckled.

Tony looked surprised as we slipped into his booth. "Hey. What's up?" he asked.

"I'll cut to the chase," I said quietly. "It's about the bandanna in your jacket pocket."

Tony's eyes darted over to his jacket. "Wh-what bandanna?" he asked with a stammer. "It must be one of my gloves."

Joe shook his head and said, "Bandannas have looked the same since the Wild West."

"Come on, Tony," I said. "Are you one of those Scaredevils?"

Tony's eyes flew wide open. He leaned across the table and whispered, "I don't belong to any gang, if that's what you're saying."

I pointed at the scratch under Tony's eye. "Then how did you get that?" I asked.

Joe was already running the fight video as he held the tablet in Tony's face. "Is this how?" he asked.

Tony stared straight at the video. "How did you find that?" he asked.

"Special delivery," Joe replied. "Were you the sender, Tony?"

Shaking his head, Tony said, "No, it must have been—"

Tony stopped midsentence.

"It must have been who?" I asked.

"Um . . . it must have been . . . someone else," Tony finished lamely.

"Come on, Tony, throw us a bone," Joe groaned. "Can't you give us a name?"

Tony hunched forward. "No, I can't."

"But you are in the Scaredevils?" Joe said.

Tony groaned as if to say, *Give me a break.* Then he whispered, "Yeah, I'm in the Scaredevils, but not because I want to trash Bayport."

Joe and I exchanged confused looks. Why else would someone join that gang unless they wanted to make trouble?

"I'm in it for the money," Tony said.

"Money?" I repeated.

"You're getting paid to do all that stuff?" Joe asked, just as surprised as I was.

"We all are," Tony explained. "Look, I am sick of wiping down dirty tables five days a week. The other day someone barfed up a whole—"

"Spare me the gross details," Joe said.

"And now I can finally get out," Tony said. "Why do you think I asked Carolyn here? For once I wanted to be able to sit back, relax, and order the most expensive stuff on the menu, like I always saw everybody else do."

Tony reached into his pocket. He pulled out a shiny silver phone and held it up. "And check out the sweet phone I was able to buy after the fight. With my busboy job it would have taken me weeks to be able to afford this," he continued.

"Yeah, okay, nice phone," Joe said. "Question is—who's been paying you and the other Scaredevils to trash Bayport?"

Tony placed his phone on the table. He leaned back and shook his head. "Sorry, guys," he said. "Can't tell."

"Why not?" I asked.

"The guy said he'd wipe tables with my face if I did," Tony said nervously. "Not worth it!"

I looked sideways at Joe, who was gazing out the window. He had to be as frustrated as I was. We'd finally pinned down a member of the Scaredevils—but he was too scared to rat on his leader.

"Uh-oh," Joe said, interrupting my thoughts. "Hey, Tony."

"What?" Tony asked.

Joe pointed at the window. "Is that your car out there getting keyed?" he asked.

"Someone's keying my car?" Tony cried.

In a flash, Tony was running up the aisle and out of the Chomp and Chew.

"Come on, Joe," I said, starting to stand. "We'd better help Tony—"

"Sit down," Joe said, picking up Tony's phone. "Now, how do you read texts on this thing?"

Texts?

"Oh, so that's your plan," I said with a grin. I turned to Chet and called, "Look out the window and let us know when Tony's coming back!"

Chet didn't ask why. He just nodded, a sweet potato fry dangling from his mouth.

"This is kind of like my tablet," Joe said as his fingers worked Tony's phone. "Got the texts. Now let's play Find the Ringleader."

"How will we know who he is?" I asked.

Joe leaned forward so I could see the phone too.

"We'll know him when we see him," Joe said. He scrolled down the texts until he reached one that read: GJ!! PU $$. "This is it!"

"Whaaaa?" I said.

I wasn't totally clueless when it came to texting—but this one was about as clear as ancient hieroglyphics.

"Allow me to translate," Joe said. "It says, 'Good job! Pick up cash.'"

"That's got to be the guy who's paying off the Scare-devils," I said. "Does it say who sent it?"

"Someone called Sylvester, C," Joe read. He looked at me questionably. "Sylvester, C . . . Sylvester, C—"

"Colin!" I blurted out as it hit me. "Joe, the text was sent by Colin Sylvester."

THE WARNING

8

JOE

"COLIN SYLVESTER?" I SAID, STARING AT the phone. "He's the ringleader of the Scaredevils?"

"He was creeping around our school right after the Scaredevils hit," Frank said. "And if anyone has the cash to pay up, it's Colin."

"Heads up, you guys," Chet hissed. "Tony's coming back."

"Drop the phone, Joe," Frank said.

"Wait," I said, my fingers fumbling on the keypad. "I have to close the texts."

After I did, I placed Tony's new phone on the table exactly where he'd left it. It was a cool phone—until we found out how he got it!

"Remember," Frank said. "Pretend to act concerned about his car."

Leaning forward and scrunching my eyebrows, I put on my best "worried" face. "So?" I asked as Tony slipped back into the booth. "How's the car?"

"Nobody keyed it," Tony said with a relieved smile. "You must have been seeing things, Hardy."

"Hey," Frank said. "Better safe than sorry."

"Especially with those Scaredevils around town," I said with a hint of sarcasm.

"Okay, are you finished asking me about the Scaredevils and the ringleader?" Tony asked. "Because I told you, I'm not spilling."

He didn't have to. After opening his texts, we had all the stuff we needed. At least for now.

"No more questions," Frank said.

"Good," Tony said, glancing over his shoulder. "Now, can you guys go back to your table? Carolyn's coming back!"

"The Scaredevils aren't your style, Tony," Frank said as we stood up. "You really ought to ditch them."

"And go back to wiping tables?" Tony said. "You think Carolyn would date a busboy?"

I wanted to say sure, but Carolyn was already at the booth. She wasn't smiling anymore, which made me wonder what Iola had told her.

Frank and I slipped back into our booth, where Iola was sipping her root beer float.

"What did you tell Carolyn about the captain of the basketball team?" I asked.

"That she got all As on her last report card," Iola said, twirling her straw in her shake. "Carolyn was totally bored, but I gave her an earful to kill time."

"Hey, it worked," Frank said. "Joe and I got some good stuff from Tony."

"You mean Tony's phone," I said, going back to my burger, which was already cold. "The Scaredevils are trashing Bayport for the money."

"And their ringleader and benefactor is Colin Sylvester," Frank added.

"You mean the rich kid?" Iola said. She shrugged. "If he's got deep pockets, then I guess it makes sense."

"Makes sense to me, too," Chet said. "Colin meant business when he hurled that soda can at me. That's one mean dude."

"Don't you think you should tell the cops about Colin?" Iola asked.

I frowned. "If only we could," I said. "But Chief Olaf doesn't listen to 'so-called detectives.'"

"Plus, we don't have any hard evidence on Colin other than that text on Tony's phone," Frank said. "And we can't get our hands on that anymore."

It made sense to me too that Colin was the Scaredevils'

ringleader. Who else would have all that money to burn? But there was still something I didn't get. . . .

"What do you think is in it for Colin?" I asked. "I mean, why would a guy who has everything want to spend his money on a bunch of stupid pranks?"

"And hang out with a bunch of Bayport High guys," Frank said. "That's what I don't get."

I watched Tony from the corner of my eye as we finished our burgers and drinks. He was smiling as he chatted up Carolyn, but every now and then his eyes would dart over to our table. When he caught me watching, he'd quickly glance away.

The guy was obviously nervous about us knowing his secret. Little did Tony know we knew more than he thought!

"Done," Frank said, pushing away his plate.

"Me too," I said. "Let's figure out the check and go."

"Why don't we just split it?" Chet said.

"Wait a minute!" I said, leaning over to read the check. "You ordered twice as much as we did, Morton—no way are we splitting it."

"But you guys ate my sweet potato fries!" Chet argued.

"Yeah, like one!" Iola said.

"Problem solved, you guys," I said, reaching for my tablet. "This thing has a calculator on it—"

CRASH!!!

My hands flew over my head as glass from the window exploded across our table. For the next few seconds, everything was a blur. People were screaming and diving under tables.

When the sound of falling glass and screams died down, I slowly and carefully looked up. Iola's hands still covered her head, while Chet crouched halfway under the table. Frank looked about as shaken up as I felt.

We weren't the only ones. I glanced around to see parents with their arms wrapped around crying kids. Customers were frantically leaving the place, forgetting to pay their bills. Others just sat frozen in stunned silence.

"Wh-what was that?" I asked, my voice shaky.

Careful not to touch the broken glass, Frank reached out and picked up the culprit. It was a medium-size rock with the word "Scaredevils" painted across it.

It was bad enough that I was getting the Scaredevil viral videos by special delivery. Now we were getting rocks hurled through nearby windows!

"Something tells me this is getting personal," I said.

"Jeez!" Chet cried, coming out from under the table. "We're not even safe at the Chomp and Chew. It's the end of civilization as we know it!"

Worried customers and waitstaff hurried over to see if we were okay. But not everyone stuck around. Tony and Carolyn were squeezing through the crowd toward the back door. Carolyn looked confused, while Tony kept glancing back nervously.

"Are you kids all right?" a worried voice asked.

I turned to see the owner of the place, Marty Rios, standing over our booth.

"We're okay," Frank said, forcing a smile.

"Two of my biggest waiters are outside trying to catch the punks," Marty said. "Whoever they are."

"Thanks, Marty," Frank said. "But I have a feeling they ran away right after they threw the rock."

"Who's they?" Marty demanded.

"The Scaredevils," Frank said, showing him the rock. "It's a gang that's pulling pranks around Bayport."

"Tell that to the police as soon as they get here," Marty suggested. "My cashier just put a call in to the station."

Marty cleared out the Chomp and Chew except for Frank and me. As we sat in another booth, waiting for the police, we talked about the case.

"Do you think Tony knew about the Scaredevils' plans?" I asked.

Frank shook his head. "He wouldn't bring Carolyn here if he did," he said. "Not exactly an awesome first date."

After a beat I turned to Frank. "So, what do you think?" I asked. "Do we tell the police what we know about Colin? Even if we don't have any proof to show them?"

"Definitely," Frank said. "One of us could have gotten seriously hurt just now . . . or even killed."

Two police officers were already at the Chomp and Chew, talking to Marty. But then the door opened wide and another walked in. My heart sank when I saw who it was.

"Olaf's in the house," I muttered.

"Great," Frank groaned.

Frank and I watched as Chief Olaf walked toward us, followed by the two officers. He was wearing his big shiny badge and his usual cynical smirk.

"Boys," Chief Olaf said with a nod. "So, tell me what you saw."

"This!" I said, showing him the rock. "It was hurled through the window we were sitting next to."

"The word 'Scaredevils' is painted on it," Frank pointed out. "It's the same gang that tagged our basketball court."

The chief took the rock from me. He turned it over in his hand before saying, "Tell me something I don't already know."

"Okay," Frank said. "We know who the ringleader of the gang is."

"How do you know?" Chief Olaf asked.

"We read it in a text," I said.

The chief held out his hand. "Can I see the text, please?" he said.

"Um . . . we don't have it," I said.

"It was on someone else's phone," Frank explained.

"Well," Chief Olaf said. "Then it won't do us much good, will it?"

"We can tell you what we found out," Frank said quickly. "For one, there's a guy paying the Scaredevils to pull the pranks."

"Paying them?" one of the officers piped up.

"Yeah!" I said. "And that person is Colin Sylvester!"

The chief's eyebrows flew up so high and fast I thought they'd hit the ceiling. Had we finally told him something he wanted to hear?

But then Chief Olaf shook his head. "It can't be Colin," he said. "Not a chance."

"Why not?" Frank asked.

"Because the Sylvesters are respected citizens of the community," Chief Olaf explained. "Their son Colin goes to Bay Academy."

"So all Bay Academy students are honest?" I asked.

I looked over at the other officers, Lasko and Fernandez, for help. They were usually friendly guys, but now they stood behind Chief Olaf, as motionless as Mount Rushmore.

"Look, boys." Chief Olaf sighed. "I am not going to bring in Colin Sylvester based on a text that I can't even read."

"But—" I started to say.

"Kids these days and their texts," Chief Olaf said to the other officers with a chuckle. "Maybe if they'd all interact more on a personal level, we wouldn't have all this trouble!"

I couldn't take it anymore. If Chief Olaf wouldn't listen to Frank and me, maybe he'd listen to Tony Riley.

"It wasn't our text, Chief Olaf," I blurted. "It was—"

"It was something we heard about," Frank cut in.

I glanced sideways at Frank. Why was he protecting Tony? If Tony knew that rock was coming, he sure did nothing to protect us!

"All we know is that the Scaredevils are starting to target Joe and me," Frank told the chief. He turned to me. "Show him the videos, Joe."

I was about to pull out my tablet when the chief held up his hand.

"Those punks are targeting the entire town of Bayport," Chief Olaf said. "So don't think you're so special, Detectives Hardy and Hardy."

"Can you at least question Colin and see what he has to say?" Frank asked.

"Absolutely not," Chief Olaf said. "There is no way I am going to embarrass good people like the Sylvesters when there's no evidence on their son."

The chief then turned to the officers and said, "Lasko, write up what the kids told us, but leave out the garbage about Colin."

"Garbage?" I gasped.

All three officers turned away from us. As they started up the aisle, Officer Fernandez glanced back and smiled. Maybe he believed us. But with Olaf as chief, did it even matter?

"Can't say we didn't try," Frank said with a sigh as we pulled on our jackets.

"Yeah," I said, giving the broken window one last look. "I guess it's up to us 'so-called detectives' to investigate Colin."

CLOSER 9

FRANK

THE LAST THING JOE AND I WANTED TO do was get up extra early the next morning—especially after that intense night at the Chomp and Chew. But if we were going to make a pit stop at Bay Academy on the way to school, we'd have to get going.

"What if we don't see Colin?" Joe asked me as I drove up Bay Academy's block.

"Maybe some of the other kids can help us out," I said.

"Other kids as in Sierra Mitchell?" Joe teased.

"I never said that," I insisted, although the thought of running into Sierra had definitely crossed my mind.

I pulled up to the curb across the street from Bay Academy.

With the other expensive student cars parked on the block, mine stuck out like a sore thumb.

As I did my best to parallel park, I caught Joe eyeing his tablet.

"What are you looking at?" I grunted as I turned the wheel. "Anything new go viral?"

Joe shook his head. "I did a search on the Sylvesters," he said. "No wonder the chief didn't want to go after them."

"What did you find?" I asked.

"The Sylvesters donated a whole chunk of money to a Bayport Police charity," Joe said.

"Money talks . . . Colin walks." I sighed.

"Speaking of Colin, I don't think we have to worry about not finding him," Joe said, pointing out the window. "Because there he goes!"

I leaned over to look out Joe's window. It didn't take long to find Colin. He was strutting confidently across the school grounds toward a group of other guys.

"Those are the guys from the Chomp and Chew," I said.

Colin and his buds fist-bumped, then exchanged words. He seemed distracted, looking past his friends to something in the school yard. I followed Colin's gaze to a bunch of girls standing a few feet away. One of those girls was Lindsay Peyton.

Joe and I watched as Colin broke away from his crew and began moving toward Lindsay. As far away as we were, I could still see Lindsay's look of disgust as he approached.

Lindsay jutted her chin in the air. She appeared to say a few angry words to Colin before huffing off with her friends.

"That girl Stacy was right," Joe said. "Lindsay can't stand Colin."

Colin glared icily at Lindsay until a slow smile spread across his face. Aunt Trudy would call it a "cat who swallowed the canary" type of smile. What was going on inside Colin's head to make him grin like that?

"We still don't know why Lindsay hates Colin," I said.

"Frank, isn't it a no-brainer?" Joe said. "The guy's a creep."

"It might be more than that," I said.

"Okay, then," Joe said. "He's a major creep!"

He reached over and blared the car horn. It caught the attention of Colin and practically all the other students.

"What are you doing?" I asked Joe.

"We came here to talk to Colin, remember?" Joe said. He then leaned out the window and shouted, "Hey, Sylvester! Can we ask you something?"

Colin grinned nastily, then yelled back, "The answer is no! You cannot switch lives with me, even for a second!"

Joe muttered something under his breath as he pushed open his door. I opened mine and stepped out too.

As we headed toward the school, we could see Colin talking to a guard. Colin turned to leave, but the guard held up his hand and called, "Excuse me. Are you Bay Academy students?"

"No, sir," I said.

"Then you can't be here," the guard said.

"If we need visitors' passes, we'd be happy to get some in the office," I said quickly.

The guard shook his head. "Sorry, boys," he said firmly. "You'll have to leave now."

Colin was back with his friends, this time smiling slyly at us. Joe was right. Colin wasn't just a creep—he was a major creep!

"You know something, Frank?" Joe said as we trudged back to our car. "I have a feeling this is going to be a bummer of a day."

I thought so too—until my phone beeped with the text that changed everything. . . .

"Okay, what's her name?" Joe teased as I smiled at my phone.

"Sierra just texted me," I said.

"She might have seen you here," Joe said. "What does she want?"

"She wants to meet me at the Meet Locker tonight," I said, still smiling as I read the text.

"You mean the coffee place?" Joe said. "I thought she didn't drink coffee."

"They serve tea, too," I said, texting back. "Twenty different kinds, as a matter of fact."

"Well, what did you tell her?" Joe asked.

"What do you think?" I said. "I said sure."

I pretended to be cool on the outside, but on the inside—cartwheels. As we stepped out of the car, Joe didn't seem so stoked anymore. In fact, he looked pretty bummed out.

"What's up?" I asked. "Don't tell me you're jealous!"

"No!" he insisted.

"Then what?" I asked.

"How did Sierra get your number?" Joe asked. "If I remember, she wrote hers on your hand. Not the other way around."

Joe had a point. How had she gotten my number? But after I thought about it, it clicked.

"We filled out those job applications at the Peytons'," I said. "We had to write our telephone and e-mail addresses on them, remember?"

"Oh yeah," Joe said, slapping his forehead.

As I adjusted the rearview mirror, I thought about my date with Sierra. First dates usually meant small talk. But this date didn't have to go that way.

"I'm going to ask Sierra about Colin tonight," I told Joe. "If she knows him from school, maybe she can give us some information."

"So this will be a working date?" Joe declared. He then smirked and said, "Yeah, right."

As I drove slowly away from Bay Academy, I took one last look at the school. Most of the kids were filing into the building, but Colin was still hanging with his friends. This time a dark-haired girl stood with them. Her back was to the street, so I couldn't see her face. I just knew it wasn't Lindsay.

"Hey, Frank," Joe said as I turned onto the highway. "I'm going to Chet's house tonight, but I want a full report after the date."

"About Colin?" I asked.

"About Sierra!" he said with a grin.

It wasn't easy focusing on school or our case the rest of the day. All I could think about was my date with Sierra. Maybe "date" was too strong a word. Maybe Sierra wanted to meet because she felt bad about what had happened at the Peytons' . . . or maybe I was overthinking the whole thing!

I got to the Meet Locker at seven forty-five and waited inside my car until four minutes past eight. Didn't want Sierra to think I was too eager—even though I was.

By the time I walked into the Meet Locker, Sierra was already there, sitting in a cushy chair and drinking a cup of tea.

"Sorry I'm late!" I blurted out as I sank into the opposite chair.

Sierra's eyes sparkled over her cup as she said, "You're not late—I'm early."

I ordered my usual iced caramel chiller. Sierra's tea smelled like vanilla. Or was that her perfume?

"This place is packed," I said.

"It usually is on a Friday night," Sierra said.

Glancing around, I wondered if there were any Scare-devils in the place. Probably not. They'd be out trashing Bayport, not sitting around sipping tea and coffee.

I turned back to Sierra. She seemed relaxed for someone working on the biggest Sweet Sixteen of the decade in just two days.

"I'm surprised you're not running around for Lindsay tonight," I said.

"Who says I'm not?" Sierra asked with a smile. "Lindsay wanted me to order a ton of coffee for her party. That's the reason I was here early."

She took another sip, then said, "So you and your brother are detectives? How did that start?"

"Our dad is a private investigator," I explained. "When Joe and I were kids, we asked a lot of questions about his cases. When he got sick of answering us, we decided to work on our own. We were only about eight and nine."

"Kid detectives?" Sierra smiled. "How sweet!"

She called me sweet! As we talked about other stuff like movies, school, and favorite foods, I started loosening up. Turns out Sierra loved mac and cheese just like me. But by the time I was on my second chiller, I decided to switch from small talk to spy talk.

"Do you know a guy at Bay Academy named Colin?" I asked.

"Colin?" Sierra said with a shrug. "There are a few guys at school named Colin."

"Colin Sylvester," I said.

Sierra put her teacup down on a side table. "Yeah, I know that Colin," she said. "He sits near me in math."

"So . . . is he bad news or what?" I asked.

Sierra blinked in surprise. "Bad news?" She chuckled. "What makes you ask that?"

I'd been hoping she wouldn't ask me that.

The friend part of me wanted to tell Sierra everything about our case—the viral videos, the vandalism. But the detective part knew not to share too much.

"Joe and I think he might be up to something," I said. "But that's all I can say for now."

"Ooh," Sierra said, her eyes flashing. "A man of mystery!"

Man of mystery. I liked that.

"Actually, Colin can be a jerk sometimes," Sierra offered. "Truth is, I think his bark is worse than his bite."

"I doubt it," I murmured, remembering the hurled soda can.

"What?" Sierra asked.

"Nothing," I said.

"By the way," Sierra chuckled, "you'll be happy to know that Mr. Peyton found a solution to Lindsay's keyed car. He bought her a new one!"

"Surprise, surprise," I laughed.

"Mr. Peyton was going to give Lindsay a new car for her sixteenth birthday anyway," Sierra said. "And speaking of the Sweet Sixteen, I'd better call it a night. I'm going to be crazy busy tomorrow with last-minute prep."

"Sure," I agreed as we stood up. "Um . . . can I call you again?"

Sierra tilted her head at me and smiled. "If I may remind you," she said, "I was the one who called you . . . so the next move is yours."

I offered to follow Sierra's car home, but she refused. She didn't seem worried about the pranks going on around Bayport. I guessed she was too busy with the party to worry about anything.

"Okay," Joe said after I picked him up at Chet's house. "So how'd it go?"

"Great!" I said as I drove the two of us home. "We talked about a lot of stuff."

"About Colin?" Joe teased. "Or about your future together?"

"Will you quit it?" I said. "I did ask Sierra about Colin, but she didn't have a lot on him. Just that he's an idiot and not dangerous."

"Glad she thinks so," Joe said. "And I'm glad you have a new girlfriend."

"Joe!" I sighed as I turned onto our block. "She's not my girl."

Yet.

As I drove up our street, I saw flashing lights in the distance.

"What's that?" I wondered.

I drove a few more feet, and then Joe said, "Frank, there's a fire truck in front of our house!"

"Fire?" I exclaimed. "No way!"

My heart pounded as I stopped behind the fire truck. Jumping out of the car, Joe and I raced toward our house. The house wasn't on fire—but our garage was.

My first feeling was relief—at least our house wasn't burning down. And since I had the car, there was nothing in the garage but some stored patio furniture and a lawn mower. But then I remembered the apartment above the garage—the apartment occupied by our aunt.

"Oh no!" I shouted. "Aunt Trudy!"

FIRED UP 10

JOE

FRANK AND I CHARGED TOWARD THE BURN-ing garage. Mom and Dad watched silently, looking very worried as the firefighters worked on the blaze.

"Mom, Dad," I said, my voice cracking. "Is Aunt Trudy up there?"

"We don't know yet," Mom said quietly. "One of the firefighters is climbing up to see."

Frank turned to me, his mouth a grim line. I didn't have to read his mind to know he was thinking the same as me: Was this the work of the Scaredevils? Were they such evil psycho creeps they would target not only Frank and me, but our family, too?

"I knew it," Dad groaned, cutting into my thoughts. "All

those smelly candles Trudy loves to burn. I warned her several times!"

"Warned me about what?" came a voice.

The four of us spun around. Standing right behind us was—

"Aunt Trudy!" Frank exclaimed.

"Where were you?" Dad asked, looking relieved.

"At the movies, seeing that new action flick," Aunt Trudy said. She stared at the now-smoldering garage. "But I guess there's more action going on here!"

Frank and I traded relieved smiles. Leave it to Aunt Trudy to crack a joke—even when her apartment was about to go up in flames. Luckily, the firefighters were getting the blaze out before it could spread that far.

Chief Madison, the fire chief, came over to us with the report.

"The garage has considerable damage," he told us. "But the apartment upstairs is unscathed."

"Great," Aunt Trudy said, walking toward the garage. "I'm going to catch up on my *Dancing with the Stars*—"

"You can watch it in the house, Trudy," Mom insisted. "Which is where you'll be staying until we know your apartment is safe."

"And no more candles," Dad said. "Please!"

Aunt Trudy flapped her hand dismissively.

"For your info, Fenton, I didn't burn any candles today," she insisted. "And if I did, I'd certainly have the brains to snuff it out before going to the movies."

"The fire couldn't have started in Aunt Trudy's apartment if there was no damage up there," I said, turning to the fire chief. "Right?"

"Right," Chief Madison agreed. "The fire started in the garage, which isn't uncommon. Lots of oily rags, clutter—"

"Sabotage," Frank cut in.

Chief Madison stared at Frank. "Excuse me?" he asked. "Did you say sabotage?"

"Someone could have set the fire as a prank," Frank said.

"Someone or someones," I agreed.

"Do you mean those kids who've been pulling pranks all over Bayport?" Mom asked. "You think they set fire to our garage?"

"They're not just any kids, Mom," I said. "They're a gang who call themselves the Scaredevils."

"We've heard about them," Chief Madison said with a frown. "But setting a fire is a lot more serious than throwing eggs down a book drop."

"Whoa," Aunt Trudy said. "Maybe I will stay in the house after all."

"We have tests to see where the fire started and how," Chief Madison said. "But it might take a few days."

He walked away to join his ladder company.

The damage wasn't too bad, but it was enough to leave the garage unusable.

"This is serious, guys," Dad said. "I think you should go to the police first thing tomorrow and tell them what you know."

"You mean talk to Chief Olaf?" I grimaced. "I'd rather get a tooth filled."

"Dad, we just told Chief Olaf we thought the Scaredevils were targeting us," Frank complained.

"We told Olaf who the ringleader was," I said. "But he didn't even listen."

Mom turned to Dad, a worried look on her face. "Maybe you should go talk to the chief, Fenton," she said. "Better yet, we both should."

"Good idea, Laura," Dad said.

Frank and I exchanged frantic looks. If Chief Olaf didn't take us seriously now, he sure wouldn't with our mommy and daddy speaking for us.

"Mom, Dad—no," I said.

"No what?" Dad asked.

"No thanks," Frank said. "Joe and I will talk to the chief tomorrow."

"But you said he won't listen to you!" Mom said.

"Oh, let them go, Laura," Aunt Trudy said, smiling in our direction. "If at first you don't succeed—try, try again!"

After the fire truck left, Frank and I climbed the stairs to our rooms. The smoke smell from the garage had wafted all the way into the house.

"Of all nights for us to be out," Frank said. "If I hadn't gone to meet Sierra, I might have caught the Scaredevils in the act."

I remembered my tablet and pulled it out. "Maybe we still can," I said. "Catch them in the act, I mean."

In Frank's room I searched YouTube for slickbro13's latest "hit." It didn't take long to find the clip I was looking for—a bunch of bandanna-wearing punks running away from our garage as the bottom edge of the door began to smolder.

"No cheering in the background this time," I pointed out. "They probably didn't want to attract Mom's and Dad's attention."

Frank moved closer to the tablet. "I did hear something on there," he said. "It sounded like someone's voice."

I replayed the clip and listened. "I don't hear anything," I admitted.

"Wait, here it comes," Frank cut in.

Quickly I turned up the volume. That's when I heard someone snicker and say, "Hah! This ought to keep the cops busy!"

That was a voice I'd know anywhere. It belonged to the gang's now infamous ringleader, Colin Sylvester!

"That's Colin on the tape, Frank," I declared. "What do you think he means about keeping the cops busy?"

"Who knows?" Frank said. "But at least we have some proof for Olaf that Colin was in on this."

"And this time," I said, smiling as I held up my tablet, "we'll convince the chief to watch the clip!"

• • •

We usually slept in on Saturdays, but this morning Frank and I were up at the crack of dawn. With Aunt Trudy now in the house, we were treated to an awesome breakfast of buckwheat pancakes and banana smoothies.

"Where'd you get these ingredients, Aunt Trudy?" Frank asked.

"I climbed the ladder up to my apartment," Aunt Trudy pretended to whisper. "Don't tell your mom and dad."

Mom and Dad came into the kitchen. When they wished Frank and me luck with Chief Olaf, I had a feeling we were going to need it—even with the clip we had of Colin at the scene of the crime.

When Frank and I arrived at the station, we walked straight to the front desk. An officer was drinking from a goofy coffee cup. On it was a pair of handcuffs and the words ONE SIZE FITS ALL.

"Good morning," Frank said. "We're here to see Chief Olaf."

Before the officer could look up from his cup, the chief himself marched right past us, followed by an angry Sanford Peyton!

"What else do you want me to do, Mr. Peyton?" Chief Olaf asked.

"Plenty!" Sanford replied. "My daughter's party is tomorrow night. You can schedule the number of officers you assured us a month ago."

"That was before all the pranks started happening around

here," Chief Olaf said. "I can't afford to put my force in one place when stores and cars are being trashed on a daily basis."

"I understand," Sanford said. "But all we have now is one officer for the whole party."

"And a good number of private security guards, I'm sure," Chief Olaf said. He gave a chuckle. "It's a Sweet Sixteen, Mr. Peyton. What's the worst that could happen—someone tries to melt the ice sculpture?"

"Funny, Olaf," Sanford said gruffly. "If this is what I pay my taxes for, I can easily retract my donation to the Bayport Police Department."

I could see the chief's face pale. He seemed to force a quick smile before saying, "Mr. Peyton, why don't we discuss this further in my office? How do you like your coffee?"

"In a French press," Sanford replied as he followed the chief through his office door. "With steamed milk, no sugar."

Frank and I watched the door slam shut. The officer looked up from his goofy cup and said, "Still want to speak to the chief?"

"Um . . . could you excuse us?" Frank said politely.

As we stepped away from the desk, I could still hear the sound of Sanford Peyton's voice arguing with the chief behind closed doors.

"Something tells me this is going to take a while," Frank said.

"Yeah." I sighed. "And who knows if the chief will even speak to us after dealing with that?"

Frank shrugged. "Maybe Mom and Dad ought to speak to the chief after all," he said. "Maybe they would have more luck."

I shook my head. "I'm not ready to go there yet," I said.

"Then what?" Frank asked, trying to keep his voice down.

"Let's find Colin and get in his face," I suggested. "We know where the Sylvesters live."

"Yeah, but how do we know Colin will be home?" Frank asked.

"It's Saturday morning, so he's probably sleeping in," I said. "Especially after a busy night of setting fires."

The chief and Sanford Peyton were still going at it when Frank and I left the police station.

"Aren't you glad we're not working that party?" Frank said to me as he drove off.

"That's for sure." I smiled. "I knew those togas were a bad sign!"

The road leading to the Sylvester house was a steep one. It wound through a wooded area until reaching a three-story glass-walled house overlooking the bay. The place looked more like a dream getaway than a family home.

"Glass walls," I observed. "Doesn't leave much to the imagination."

Frank parked at a safe distance.

As we quietly walked toward the house, I couldn't help

but wonder what Colin was dreaming about as he slept in. More fires? A detonation somewhere? The possibilities were endless in a sick mind like his!

Once at the house, Frank and I got nosy. We peered through the glass into what looked like the Sylvesters' den. But unlike most dens, the walls weren't lined with bookshelves or entertainment equipment. These walls were covered with guns and rifles!

"Will you look at that?" I whispered.

"There must be two dozen guns in there," Frank whispered back. "Some look like antiques. One looks as old as the Civil War."

"That's a lot of coinage," I said.

"Whatever they're worth, it's probably lunch money for the Sylvesters," Frank scoffed.

I couldn't take my eyes off the guns. Why did the Sylvesters have them hanging in plain sight like that? As a warning to home invaders? Or to snoopers like Frank and me?

"Joe!"

"What?" I said, turning to Frank.

"Colin is out on his deck," he said. "I can see him through the glass."

"That's what we're here for," I said. "Let's go over to him and—"

"He's with his friends," Frank finished.

"Oh," I said.

I peered through the glass all the way out to the deck.

There was Colin, leaning back in an Adirondack chair and eating what looked like a muffin. Standing around him and drinking coffee were the same guys from his school.

"Five against two?" I said with a sigh. "I think this calls for a change of plans."

"Let's go around the house," Frank said. "Maybe we can hear what they're talking about."

Sticking close to the wall, we moved toward the back where the deck stood. When we got to the end of the wall, we stopped and strained our ears to listen. We heard a few words thrown around but couldn't make out the conversation.

"This isn't going to work," Frank murmured.

I was about to agree until I remembered something inside my jacket pocket—the ear amplifier Connie had given me at Dad's office.

"Let's see if this thing works," I whispered. After untangling the wire, I stuck the bud in my right ear. Yes! The voices of Colin Sylvester and his peeps were coming in loud and clear!

I gave Frank a thumbs-up, then listened closely.

"I wish you could taste how awesome this muffin is," Colin was saying. "The blueberries are, like, the size of my fist."

I rolled my eyes. Colin's breakfast? Was this how good it was going to get?

"What?" Frank hissed, dying to know what I heard.

Suddenly I heard a girl's voice speak up. It sounded scratchy, as if it was coming through a speakerphone. It also sounded familiar.

"So tell me about the plan," she said. "How's it coming along?"

"The plan is going according to plan!" Colin chuckled. "Trust me, babe. Soon it'll all be worth it."

"Yeah!" one of his friends said. "This is going to be huge!"

Frank must have seen my eyes pop wide open. "What?" he whispered. "What are you hearing?"

I shook my head as if to say, *Wait*. It was the girl's voice I heard next.

"Colin, you are soooo bad," she said. "But that's why you're my guy."

I yanked out the earbud and turned to Frank. "Colin is planning something big," I whispered. "And it's going down soon."

"A plan?" Frank whispered. "What kind of plan?"

"Don't know." I shrugged.

"That's it," Frank said, no longer whispering. "I don't care that he's with his friends. We're questioning him right now—"

"Hello," a voice said.

Frank and I spun around. A tanned, middle-aged woman wearing a white tennis outfit was standing a few feet away.

"G-good morning!" Frank stammered.

"Um . . . Mrs. Sylvester?" I asked.

"Mrs. Sylvester?" She laughed. "All of Colin's friends call me Barbara."

"I meant . . . Barbara!" I said, laughing too. All the time my heart was pounding inside my chest. Had Colin's mom seen us snooping around? Had she caught the listening device in my ear?

"Why don't I tell Colin you're here?" Barbara Sylvester said, heading toward the deck. "I can get Helga to bring out more muffins."

"No!" Frank said quickly. "I mean, thanks, but we were just leaving."

"The muffins were great, by the way," I said. "Blueberries the size of my fist!"

I felt Barbara's eyes on us as we hurried back to our car.

"That was close," Frank said.

"Yeah, but what happened to questioning Colin?" I asked.

"I'm not questioning anyone in front of his mom," Frank said as we climbed back into the car. "So how soon is this plan going down? Did anyone say?"

"No, but I found out something else," I said.

"What?" Frank asked.

"It sounded like Colin Sylvester has a girlfriend," I said. "He was talking to her on speakerphone."

"A girlfriend?" Frank scoffed as he turned the key. "Anyone interested in that guy has got to be bad news too."

"That's for sure," I agreed. "What do you think this 'huge' plan of his is, Frank?"

Frank sighed as he turned the car around. "I don't know," he said. "But whatever it is—it can't be good."

CHANGE OF PLANS

11

FRANK

AS I DROVE FARTHER AWAY FROM THE Sylvester house, I couldn't stop thinking about this plan Joe had heard about.

How would we stop it when we didn't know what it was?

"Frank," Joe interrupted my thoughts. "That girl on the speakerphone . . ."

"What about her?" I asked.

"Her voice sounded familiar," Joe said.

I shot him a sideways glance. He was staring out the passenger window, deep in thought.

"You mean like someone from school?" I asked. "If she's Colin's girl, chances are she goes to Bay Academy."

"Then I wouldn't know her," Joe said, shrugging it off.

"It's eleven o'clock. Do you think it's too early for pizza?"

"For you, no," I said. "For me, yes."

"Think of it as a power lunch," Joe said. "While we feast on pepperoni and mushrooms, we can talk about the case."

We had a lot to talk about, especially after what we'd heard at Colin's.

"You win," I said, turning the car onto Bay Street. "Pizza, here we come."

Saturday was the busiest shopping day of the week, so I was lucky to find a parking spot right away.

"Let's go to Pie Squared, the place that makes those square-shaped pizzas," Joe suggested.

"Are the pepperoni square too?" I joked.

Joe was too busy staring up the street to get my joke.

"What is it?" I asked.

"Check out who's coming," Joe said.

Turning my head, I saw who Joe was talking about. Strutting toward us and swinging shopping bags from both hands was Lindsay Peyton. She was walking next to another girl, also armed with bags.

"Good timing," I said. "Let's see what she knows about Colin."

It wasn't sunny, but the two girls were wearing huge dark sunglasses. One of Lindsay's bags smacked into my leg as the two breezed by.

"Hey!" Joe called after them. "Remember us?"

Lindsay peered over her shoulder. "Oh, it's you two," she said in a voice as cold as ice.

"I've heard friendlier greetings at the Haunted Mansion," Joe said as we walked over.

"It happened to be an appropriate one," Lindsay said, raising her chin. "You know, my dad had to get me a new car."

She turned to her friend and said, "Not that that was a bad thing, right, Grace?"

"Right!" Grace laughed.

The friends readied to high-five, only to realize their hands were full.

"If you're still saying we keyed your car, you're wrong," I said. "It was already keyed when we got to the parking lot."

"Whatever," Lindsay said with a shrug.

"You heard about all that gang stuff going around, didn't you?" Joe asked.

Lindsay stared at him. "Are you serious?" she said. "Do you know what tomorrow is?"

"Sunday?" Joe said.

"Omigosh, tomorrow is Lindsay's Sweet Sixteen!" Grace said as if we'd just touched down from another planet.

"Who has time to think about anything else?" Lindsay asked. She tilted her head and said, "So are you kicking yourself for not working my party?"

Joe shook his head. "Togas aren't my style."

Lindsay clicked her tongue in disgust. She and Grace were about to turn when I said, "Wait!"

I couldn't let Lindsay leave before asking her about Colin.

"I heard you didn't invite Colin Sylvester to your party," I said quickly.

Lindsay's shoulders drooped at the mention of Colin. "Did he tell you that?" she asked.

"No," I said. "We must have overheard it somewhere. Can't remember where or when—"

"We just want to know why he's not invited," Joe cut in. "That's all."

Lindsay pushed her sunglasses up on her head. She narrowed her eyes and said, "Because Colin Sylvester is a psycho creep—that's why!"

"Colin's been trying to ask Lindsay out since middle school," Grace said. "He even tried to get into our clique at school."

"And you kept turning him down?" I asked Lindsay.

"I wouldn't go out with Colin if he looked like an Abercrombie model," Lindsay snapped. "I'm just glad he has a girlfriend now—maybe he'll leave me alone."

"Who is she?" Joe asked.

"Who?" Lindsay repeated.

"Colin's girlfriend," Joe urged.

"Is she bad news like him?" I asked.

Lindsay wrinkled her nose and said, "What are you guys—some kind of investigative reporters?"

"Sort of," Joe said.

"Whatever, I can't talk now," Lindsay said impatiently,

dropping her sunglasses over her eyes. "I have a ton of stuff to do before my party tomorrow."

"Like having your eyebrows waxed in ten minutes!" Grace reminded her.

"Gracie!" Lindsay complained as the two hurried away. "Like, thanks for letting them think I have a unibrow!"

When the girls were out of earshot, I said, "Well, I guess it's true that Lindsay hates Colin—he sounds like a creep."

We continued up the block, and Joe said, "Frank, do you think Colin's big plan includes the Scaredevils?"

"Probably," I said. "The Scaredevils seem to be Colin's sock puppets. They'll do anything for his money."

"And I'll do anything for pizza right now," Joe said. "You know I can't talk about a case on an empty stomach."

"Okay, okay," I said, smiling. "We're almost there."

Joe and I made our way to Pie Squared, where we shared a pepperoni pizza with olives and mushrooms.

"So," Joe said, popping a mushroom into his mouth. "What's next on the agenda?"

I wanted to answer him, but not with a big piece of mozzarella cheese hanging from my mouth over my chin. I must have looked pretty pathetic, especially when the door opened and in walked—of all people—Sierra Mitchell!

I yanked the cheese from my mouth—only to get it tangled around my hand.

"Hey, guys!" Sierra called with a wave.

"Smooth, bro, real smooth," Joe teased.

When my hand was finally cheese free, I smiled coolly and said, "Hey."

"Don't tell me you eat pizza for breakfast too," Joe said to Sierra.

"No," Sierra said. "I'm actually here on a work mission. The party planners are toiling around the clock for Lindsay's Sweet Sixteen tomorrow, so we all need lunch."

"We're working today too," I said. "Those pranks around Bayport are keeping us busy."

"Oh, that's right, you're detectives," Sierra said. She then planted her hands on her hips and added, "Well, if you ask me, I think we're all working a little too hard for a Saturday."

"It is what it is," Joe said with a shrug.

"We can still take a break," Sierra said. Her eyes lit up. "Why don't you come over to the Peytons', Frank, and we'll take one of their boats out for a spin?"

"So Mr. Peyton can accuse us of trying to steal his boat?" I scoffed. "Thanks—but no thanks."

"Borrowing the boat is one of my job perks," Sierra explained. "I get to use the small powerboat during my breaks."

"Not the yacht?" I joked.

"Maybe when I become head event planner," Sierra joked back. "But for now the small boat is cool. I took it out yesterday afternoon and had a blast."

I smiled at the thought of boating with Sierra—until I felt Joe kick me under the table and give me a look. Now what?

"I know," Sierra said excitedly. "Why don't you come with us, Joe?"

"Me?" Joe asked, surprised.

"Him?" I asked, even more surprised.

"The more the merrier," Sierra said cheerily.

"In that case," Joe said, "thanks!"

"Yeah, thanks," I muttered to Joe. Better than nothing, I guess.

"Super!" Sierra said as she glanced at her watch. "Meet me at the Peytons' docks at two o'clock. Just go around the house to the back and I'll be there."

Sierra then did something totally unexpected. She threw me a kiss before walking to the take-out counter. Me—not Joe!

"I saw that," Joe teased again. "She's got it bad for you, big brother."

We finished our pizza, then got ready to go boating. I changed into khaki shorts, a polo shirt, and flip-flops. Joe pulled on a pair of cleaner jeans, sneakers, and a T-shirt sporting a soft-drink logo.

"You look like you go to Bay Academy!" Joe joked when we reached the Peyton house.

"And you look like you're in kindergarten!" I complained.

There was no Peyton sighting as we headed around the house to the two docks.

"Can you imagine what Sanford would do if he saw us trespassing like this?" Joe asked as we walked down a hill toward the bay.

"We're not trespassing," I reminded him. "Taking out the boat is one of Sierra's job perks. She told us herself."

"So where is Sierra?" Joe asked, looking around. "She told us she'd meet us here."

I didn't see Sierra either. Were we about to get stood up?

Joe whistled through his teeth as he moved up the docks. "Hey—check out Sanford's awesome toys," he said.

There were three boats roped along the two docks—two luxury cabin cruisers and a smaller powerboat with a sleek V-shaped hull. Not too shabby, to say the least.

"Frank, Joe," Sierra's voice called.

I smiled when I saw Sierra at the top of the hill, but my good mood quickly faded. She looked upset.

"What's up?" I called up to her.

"My supervisor just called," Sierra said, her shoulders drooping. "She wants me to order a limo for the band."

"So you can't go boating?" Joe asked.

"Not right now," Sierra said. "Why don't you take the powerboat out in the meantime? I'll meet you back on the dock in twenty minutes."

"It's okay," I said. "We'll wait for you—"

"No!" Sierra said kind of quickly. "Take the boat out, so I won't feel so guilty. When was the last time you drove a boat?"

"Last summer," I said. "I have my license and everything."

"Great," Sierra said, tossing me the key. "See you in twenty minutes, okay?"

"Okay!" I called back.

Sierra ran back to the house.

"I guess we're on our own," I said as I walked up the dock to Joe. "At least for now."

Joe was already untying the powerboat. "All right!" he exclaimed. "Joy ride, baby!"

As I walked up to the boat, I felt a little uneasy. Sure, it was pretty cool to take it for a spin, but I didn't think Mr. Peyton would feel the same way. When I told Joe my thoughts, he waved me off.

"He'll never know," he assured me as he stepped in.

Let's hope he doesn't, I thought.

It took us a few minutes to untie the boat. Once it was freed from the dock, we climbed inside.

"I'll drive," I said, taking my place behind the wheel. Joe sat next to me, slipping on a pair of shades.

Before I started the engine, I did a few safety checks. There was plenty of fuel. Check. Life jackets. Check.

After a few more checks, I turned on the ignition switch. When I pulled back on the throttle, it felt loose, but it didn't seem to be an issue as I cast the boat off from the dock. After turning the craft around, I pushed the throttle forward.

"Full speed ahead!" I exclaimed as the boat cut across the water at an exhilarating pace.

"Woo-hooo!" Joe cheered.

I had forgotten what a blast boating could be—especially knowing we'd have another pretty passenger joining us soon.

But my thoughts were interrupted by the roar of a Jet Ski engine.

Turning my head, I saw the Jet Ski in the distance, heading right into our path.

"Slow down so you don't hit her," Joe said.

"Duh!" I responded as I grabbed the throttle. But as I pulled back on the throttle, something happened that turned my blood to ice.

The handle came off in my hand!

"Frank, slow down!" Joe cried, his eyes still on the Jet Ski. "We're going to crash!"

"I can't, Joe!" I shouted, staring at the handle in my hand. "I can't!"

ROUGH SEAS

12

JOE

I N A PANIC, FRANK FUMBLED TO POP THE THROTTLE back in, only to watch it pop out again.

"Turn around!" I started yelling at the jet skier. "Turn around!"

By now I was standing up in the boat, my head spinning. We were either going to crash into the Jet Ski or into some trees on the opposite bank. Just as I was about to brace for the worst, I remembered another way to stop.

"The key!" I shouted.

My hand jutted out and turned the ignition key. The boat sputtering to a stop was like music to my ears. I could hear Frank heave a sigh as he slumped back on the seat.

The jet skier zoomed past us, just a few feet away. "When

are you going to learn how to drive?" she shouted above the whirring engine.

"When you learn how to turn that thing around!" I shouted back angrily.

"I think I'm going to barf," Frank groaned slowly.

Picking up the fallen throttle, I shook my head. "I hope the Peytons get a refund on this hunk of junk."

"I don't get it," Frank said. "How could a boat that must have cost hundreds of thousands of dollars fall apart like some kid's toy?"

"Whatever happened, we'd better find a way to put this thing back where it belongs so we can get back to the dock!" I said.

As I leaned over to check the throttle, something caught my eye. On the floor of the boat, tucked deep under the dashboard, were a bunch of loose screws and a screwdriver.

Picking up one of the screws, I sized it up with the throttle. A perfect fit!

"Something tells me this wasn't an accident, Frank," I said.

"Wait a minute," he said. "Are you saying someone unscrewed the throttle before we got into the boat?"

"It's possible," I said.

"But I used the throttle to cast off," Frank said.

We studied the throttle. The most likely explanation was that only part of it had been unscrewed before we got into the boat. It would have been just a matter of time before the whole thing would pop off—which it had.

"Looks like somebody was trying to hurt the Peytons," I said. "Or us."

"Us?" Frank repeated.

"The Scaredevils already got to us," I said. "The fire, the rock through the window . . ."

"How would they know we were going boating?" Frank asked. "The only one who knew was Sierra, and we know she isn't a Scaredevil."

Maybe not. But something about Sierra was starting to feel sketchy to me. Like, why had she invited Frank out at the last minute the night of the fire? And why had she invited both of us boating when the boat was unsafe?

Frank must have noticed me deep in thought, because he raised his eyebrow and said, "What?"

"Nothing," I said. "Let's just fix this thing so we can get back."

"Yeah," Frank said. "Sierra's probably wondering where we are."

We used the screwdriver to reattach the throttle handle. When we were sure it was safe, Frank turned the boat around and drove toward the dock—slowly this time!

"I think I know how this happened," Frank said as the boat bounced over the rippling currents.

"How?" I asked.

"The Peytons could have had someone working on the boat before we took it out," Frank explained. "Sierra might not have even known it."

"Didn't she say she took the boat out yesterday afternoon?" I reminded. "She didn't mention anything being wrong with it then."

Frank rolled his eyes. "Someone could have noticed the problem this morning," he said.

"Right," I murmured, but I didn't buy it. The whole thing smelled of sabotage to me, but Frank was way too in love to get a whiff.

As the boat approached shore I could see Sierra, waving both hands in the air.

"Are you guys okay?" Sierra called out. "It looked like you were fixing something on the boat!"

Frank nodded as we climbed out onto the dock. "We're fine," he said. "We just had a little . . . mechanical difficulty."

"Mechanical difficulty," I muttered. "Yeah, you could say that."

I got a hard glare from Frank, telling me to shut up. He then smiled at Sierra and said, "Did you finish your work? That order you had to call in?"

She nodded and said, "I got the extra flowers we needed."

"Flowers?" I said, tilting my head. "I thought you had to order a limo for the band."

Sierra blinked fast before saying, "I did. Then I got a text from my boss telling me to order more flowers."

I frowned. Was she lying to us?

"Where's Mr. Peyton?" I asked.

"Why do you want to know?" Sierra asked.

"I want to tell him somebody messed with his boat, that's why," I said.

"You don't have to tell Mr. Peyton," Sierra blurted out.

"Why not?" I asked.

"Joe . . . ," Frank started to say.

"Because while I was inside, I found out there was a problem with the boat," Sierra said. "I tried to stop you from going out, but it was too late."

"Who told you about the boat?" I asked.

"Joe, will you quit it?" Frank snapped. "She's trying to explain what happened."

Sierra glared at me. "Why does it matter who told me?" she demanded. "You wouldn't know him anyway."

"So introduce us!" I said with a shrug.

"You don't believe me, do you?" Sierra demanded. "What do you think—that I messed with the boat?"

"Forget it, Sierra," Frank said gently. "Joe is just shaken up from the whole thing."

"Shaken up?" I cried.

"This boating idea was a bad one, Frank," Sierra said. "I'm sorry I suggested it."

"No, it was a great idea!" Frank said. "Maybe we can do it another time?"

"Yeah, like when the boat's safe?" I added, before Frank gave me a shove.

"We'll definitely do it another time," Sierra said directly to Frank. "But just the two of us, okay?"

Without looking at me, Sierra turned to walk back to the house.

"Okay, what was that all about?" Frank demanded.

I waited until Sierra was back inside before saying, "You tell me, Frank. Are you so into Sierra you refuse to call her out on her stuff?"

"What stuff?" Frank cried. "She told us the boat was busted before we got in."

"I'm not sure I buy it," I admitted. "And I'm starting to have bad feelings about Sierra, Frank. Sorry, but I do."

"Yeah, well, I have feelings for her too," Frank said. "And FYI, they're all good."

"Does that mean you're not buying my sabotage theory?" I asked. "Any of it?"

"Only if the Scaredevils knew we were going boating," Frank said. "And I can't imagine how they would."

"That's why we're going to track down Colin," I insisted. "I don't care if he's with his friends or his great-grandmother— we're going to question him until he's blue in the face."

I could see Frank was disappointed as we walked back to the car. But just as he started unlocking the car door, he got a text.

"Who's it from?" I asked.

Frank's eyes widened as he read the message. "It's from Chet," he said. "He wants us to come over ASAP."

"Did he say why?" I asked.

"It's the Scaredevils," Frank said, looking up from the phone. "They got to Iola."

TWISTS AND TURNS

13

FRANK

I T WAS HARD NOT TO GO OVER THE SPEED LIMIT as Joe and I drove to Chet's house. The text hadn't explained what had happened to Iola, so we could only think the worst.

"Why would the Scaredevils want to do something to Iola?" Joe asked as I careened into the Mortons' driveway.

"Because she's our friend?" was all I could guess. "And any friend of ours is probably an enemy of theirs."

Chet was already at the door as we raced up to the house. "Hey," he said.

"How's Iola?" I asked.

"She's in the living room," Chet said, opening the door wider to let us inside. "See for yourselves."

Joe and I headed down the hallway. We turned into the

living room to see Iola sitting on the sofa. She looked okay, but was she really?

"Hi," Iola said, looking up from a magazine she was reading.

"Just hi?" Joe asked. "What happened?"

"Nothing." Iola sighed. "I'm fine."

"She thinks it's nothing," Chet said. "But Iola was in a fight."

Iola rolled her eyes. "Almost a fight, Chet," she said. "Will you stop being the overprotective big brother and give me some space?"

"Tell us what happened!" I urged Chet.

Chet turned to us, his face grim. "Some girls wearing blue bandannas over their faces started picking on Iola as she was walking home from her friend's house," he explained.

"What did they do to you?" I asked Iola.

"It didn't go anywhere," Iola explained. "Even though half their faces were covered, I recognized two of them from school. When I called them out, they turned and ran away."

"Good thing," Chet said.

"Do you know where they went?" Joe asked.

Iola shrugged and said, "Up the block, then around the corner."

I was still trying to process the whole thing. "I didn't know girls were in the Scaredevils," I said.

"I guess they need the money too," Joe said. He shook his head. "Man, whatever happened to flipping burgers and babysitting?"

The money made me think of the Scaredevils' benefactor—Colin Sylvester.

"Was anyone else there?" I asked Iola. "Any guys?"

"No," Iola said, but quickly added, "Yes . . . well, maybe."

"Jeez, Iola!" Chet complained. "Is it yes, no, or maybe so?"

"I'm not sure," Iola said. "There was a black car parked on the block. After the girls ran off, the car took off too, practically speeding."

"Could you see who was inside?" Joe asked.

"No, but I remember his plate," Iola said. "It said something like Awesome . . ."

"Awesome Dude!" I declared. "Better known as Colin Sylvester."

"Him?" Iola wrinkled her nose. "That creep was in the car watching us all that time? Eww."

"I'll bet he taped the whole thing too," Joe said. "It's probably gone viral by now."

"But nothing happened," Iola said.

Chet was already on the computer, browsing YouTube. He held it up and said, "Here it is. Slickbro13's latest viral venture."

"Slickbro13 . . . Awesome Dude?" Iola scoffed. "The guy obviously has no self-esteem issues."

We huddled around the computer to check out the video. Colin's shaky camera caught the Scaredevils approaching Iola, but ended right before they bolted.

"There's no audio on this one," Joe pointed out.

"No surprise," Iola said. "I said the girls' names—Amy and Desiree."

"It's a good thing you did," Chet said. "Who knows what could have happened if you didn't recognize them?"

Iola patted Chet's shoulder. "Thank you for your concern, big brother," she said. "But I'm okay. Really."

We were all glad Iola was okay. But the thought of Colin pitting his gang against our friends made me want to hunt him down even more. How could we even think of going boating when he was still on the loose?

"Tonight we find Mr. Awesome Dude," I told Joe. "Once and for all."

"Tonight?" Joe exclaimed. "Why don't we go to his house right now?"

"Because we promised Dad we'd help him fix up the garage for a bit, remember?" I reminded him. "And tonight is Saturday night. Everyone will be out, especially the Scaredevils. And where there're Scaredevils, there's Colin."

Joe nodded thoughtfully. "Tonight could be the night Colin carries out his big plan," he said.

"Yeah, well, we have a plan too," I said, glaring at the YouTube clip on Chet's computer.

Fixing up our fire-wrecked garage was grueling work, and it would take more than a few hours to finish the job. By the time we stopped for the day, Joe and I were ready to take on another wreck—Colin Sylvester!

But first . . . we had to be excused from dinner.

"What do you mean, you won't be home for dinner?" Mom asked. "Your dad is grilling some steaks."

"Save us some leftovers, please," Joe said. "We'll be hungry when we get back."

The last thing we wanted to do was worry Mom or Dad with the details. All we wanted to do was wait outside the Sylvester home for Colin. As soon as his car left the house, we wouldn't be too far behind.

"I'm getting hungry," Joe said after about an hour of watching for Colin. "Maybe we should have taken some food for the road. Steak for a stakeout . . . get it?"

"Got it," I groaned as I slumped back on the seat. My eyes burned from looking for Colin in the dark. "Maybe this wasn't such a great idea."

My phone beeped. Another text from Chet. Had the Scaredevils come back for Iola? Or for him? But when I read his message, it was good news, or at least helpful.

"Chet said he just spotted Colin's car parked at the Cineplex," I said, sitting up straight again. "The Awesome Dude plate gave it away."

"Perfect!" Joe said with a grin. "I'd rather stake him out at the movies than here."

"What's the difference?" I asked.

"Three words," Joe said. "Take-out food!"

Awesome Dude's black Benz was still parked at the Cineplex when we arrived. We were able to find a spot close to Colin's car but not close enough for him to see us waiting.

"I wonder what movie Colin is seeing," I said.

"Probably one that makes him laugh," Joe said with a smirk. "Like a slasher movie."

Joe browsed his tablet for movie times. "The next movie ends in forty-five minutes," he said. "Plenty of time to grab some grub."

My stomach was starting to growl too, so we left the car for the Stop and Snack. The convenience store did a good business, being right next to the Cineplex. It was owned by Bruce and Sheila Davis, a cool couple who were there most of the twenty-four hours it was open.

But as Joe and I walked inside, something felt and looked different. The place wasn't packed with the usual moviegoers. It was just Bruce, Sheila, and two police officers.

Sheila saw us and waved. "Come on in, guys," she called. "Everything's back on the shelves now. We're taking customers again."

"Back on the shelves?" Joe murmured as we stepped inside. "That doesn't sound good."

The police officers walked past Joe and me on their way out of the store.

"What do you mean, you're taking customers again?" I asked the Davises. "What happened?"

"Ah, some crazy kids were in here a couple of hours ago," Bruce said. "They were running up and down the aisles and knocking stuff off the shelves."

"No way!" I gasped. A few hours ago it was still light out. If it was the Scaredevils, they were getting bold.

"Were they wearing blue bandannas?" Joe asked. "Over their faces?"

"Yeah," Bruce said. He raised an eyebrow. "How did you guys know?"

"It's the same gang that's been trashing Bayport the last few weeks," I explained.

"I know all about those pranks," Sheila said, shaking her head. "I'm sure the cops are working hard, but when are they going to catch those punks?"

"Probably when they catch the ringleader," I replied.

As we walked over to the pretzels and chips Joe whispered, "You mean when *we* catch the ringleader."

We bought a medium-size bag of honey-mustard pretzels and two cold lemonades. As we walked back to the parking lot, Joe suddenly said, "Frank—over there!"

Joe's hands were full, so he pointed with his elbow. I turned to see Colin walking away from the Cineplex, his arm around a girl.

"I guess he didn't stay for the credits," I said, narrowing my eyes. "Come on. Let's let him know we're here."

Colin was already in the car as we got near.

"Spare me," I groaned. "Colin and his girl are kissing."

Joe's eyes suddenly grew wide.

"What?" I asked.

"Get back here," Joe said. He darted behind a Dumpster

directly in front of Colin's car. I joined him there as he placed our snacks on the ground.

"So what are we doing?" I asked.

"This is the perfect place to spy on them," Joe said, his voice low.

"You mean spy on them kissing?" I cried. "What are we, in grade school? We should be pinning Colin against his car, demanding answers!"

"We will," Joe said as he peeked out from behind the Dumpster. "First I want to see who the girl is."

"It's too dark to see anything, Joe," I said. "And who cares who she is?"

Another car drove by. Its headlights illuminated the area, including Colin's car. For a split second I was able to see the girl as she leaned back against the car seat and smiled. My heart sank like a stone when I suddenly realized who she was. It was Sierra!

DECEPTION 14

JOE

"OH, MAN, FRANK," I SAID WITH A SIGH. "Sorry."

Frank seemed too stunned to say a word. It was then that I realized why the voice on Colin's phone had sounded so familiar. I also realized why I'd had those weird feelings about Sierra. Not only was she Colin's girlfriend, she was probably his spy!

"Frank?" I said, looking over at him. He wasn't peering out from behind the Dumpster anymore. He was sitting on the ground, slumped against it. "Frank, are you okay?"

Frank stared straight ahead. "Looks like your bad feelings about Sierra were right," he muttered.

"Hey," I said with a shrug. "A lucky guess."

I turned back to the car. Colin and Sierra were kissing

117

again—the perfect time to catch them by surprise.

"Come on, Frank!" I said. "Let's surprise them."

He shook his head. "Colin's in his car. He'll either take off—or knowing him, run us over."

"But we have enough time to get our car," I said. "As long as they're still kissing—"

Frank glared at me.

Oops.

"Okay, I'll shut up," I said. "But we're wasting precious time here!"

I turned back toward the car. Colin and Sierra had stopped kissing and were talking now. After sharing a laugh, they high-fived. Were they talking about the plan? The car windows were open, but they were too far away for us to hear a thing.

. . . Or were they?

I reached for the amplifier, still in my jacket pocket. I stuck it in my ear, but this time heard nothing.

"Arrrgh!" I said. "The battery must have died."

The sudden sound of an engine made me jump. I yanked out the earbud just as Colin's headlights flashed, illuminating the Dumpster and us. I ducked behind the Dumpster. Was it too late? Had Colin or Sierra seen us?

With a loud screech, the car backed out of the parking lot. It turned, then roared off.

"Frank, let's chase them," I said. "If we get to our car in time, we might have a chance—"

"Forget it, Joe," Frank said. "They're already out of the lot."

"So, what, we're not even going to try?" I cried.

"Not with Sierra in the car," Frank said. He then shook his head and murmured, "Sierra and Colin. Unbelievable."

I sank down next to Frank. I took a noisy slurp of my lemonade and said, "I kind of believe it. Remember how she invited you out last night, the night of the fire?"

"What are you saying?" Frank asked. "That she wanted to get me out of the way so the Scaredevils could burn our garage?"

"That—or get information from you," I said. "Maybe Colin wanted to know how much we knew about him and the gang."

"Great," Frank grumbled.

"I'll bet that's how the Scaredevils got my e-mail address," I figured. "Sierra took it from the job application I filled out."

I knew Frank didn't want to hear it, but I had to go on about Sierra.

"Sierra invited us on that boat," I said. "Probably knowing that it was rigged by Colin—or maybe herself."

"It's my fault," Frank said, standing up. "I told Sierra about the case we were working on, so the Scaredevils came after us."

"It wasn't your fault, Frank," I said.

"Sure it was," he said angrily. "Sierra played me, and I fell for it."

We carried our drinks and pretzels back to our car. Frank didn't say a word.

"Frank," I said, "how do you think someone like Sierra got a job working for the Peytons?"

"Sierra's obviously good at deceiving people," Frank said bitterly. "She could be playing the Peytons too."

Playing the Peytons?

The idea made me stop in my tracks.

"Maybe Sierra isn't there to help plan Lindsay's Sweet Sixteen," I told Frank. "Maybe she's there to help Colin bring down Lindsay's Sweet Sixteen!"

Frank shot me a puzzled look.

"Think about it, Frank," I continued. "Colin wasn't invited to the party of the decade. A guy like him wouldn't take that lightly."

"Especially since Lindsay's been rejecting him since middle school," Frank agreed.

"Not only did she reject him," I said, "she kept him from being a part of her clique."

"So trashing Lindsay's Sweet Sixteen makes sense to him," Frank said.

"I just can't figure out what the Scaredevils have to do with the party," I said slowly. "You know, all those pranks that went viral."

Frank took a long sip of his lemonade. I could tell he was thinking hard from the way his eyes darted back and forth. Suddenly both eyes snapped wide open. He turned to me and said, "Joe, do you remember what Colin said in that video?"

"Which one?" I asked.

"The one where we heard his voice in the background," Frank said. "He said, 'This ought to keep the cops busy.'"

"Yeah . . . so?" I asked.

"Remember when Sanford Peyton came to the police station?" Frank said. "He was complaining that there weren't enough cops scheduled for Lindsay's party."

"Yeah!" I said, the pieces starting to come together. "Colin was keeping the cops busy with the Scaredevils' pranks so they'd be too busy to cover Lindsay's Sweet Sixteen."

"And if Colin is planning on trashing it," Frank said, "the fewer cops, the more trouble!"

It made total sense to me now. Trashing Lindsay's Sweet Sixteen was the perfect act of revenge. And if anyone seemed the vengeful type, it was Colin Sylvester.

"Okay," I said. "Now that we've figured out Colin's plan—what's ours?"

Frank took another long sip of his lemonade. He then looked me straight in the eye.

"If Colin is planning to trash the party," he said, "then we're going to crash the party."

"I thought you wanted to work this Sweet Sixteen, Chet," I said.

"Not wrapped in a sheet, dudes," Chet groaned. "I feel like a pig in a blanket without the mustard!"

It was early Sunday night. Frank, Chet, and I had parked all the way down the hill from the Bayport Bijou, the hall where Lindsay's Sweet Sixteen was about to rock. We spent the whole day mapping out our plan and suiting up for the party we were about to crash. And that meant togas.

"We told you a million times, Chet," Frank said as we trudged up the hill. "These costumes are the best way to sneak into the party. It's what all the waiters will be wearing."

"I doubt they got theirs on sale at Sid's Novelty Shop," I said. Then, striking my best ancient-Roman-senator pose, I added, "So, do I look like Caesar?"

"With those leaves around your head?" Chet snorted. "More like Caesar salad."

I gazed upward. Besides the head wreath, the costume came with fake leather sandals, a white tunic, and a gold sash. Sid threw in some freebies—fake gold wrist and ankle cuffs.

"I just wish these things had pockets," I complained. "Where am I going to keep my tablet?"

Chet tugged at his waist pouch. "I'll carry it for you in here, Joe," he said. "I brought it for leftover party food."

We reached the top of the hill to look out at the Bayport Bijou. Valets were busy parking classy cars as they drove up to the entrance one by one. Blinged-out guests strutted up the lantern-lit path like celebs on the red carpet.

"Serious bling going in there, dudes," Chet said. "If crazy Colin is planning a heist, he's coming to the right place."

I hoped Colin would show up. Frank and I were going on

a hunch, and as good as it was, it was still just a hunch.

"It looks like the staff is entering through the side," Frank said, pointing to some other toga-sporting guys. "Let's give it a shot."

We walked toward the building, trying our best to look like we belonged.

"I just had a bad thought," Frank murmured. "What do we do if Sierra sees us? She knows we're not working the party."

I shook my head. "There are over two hundred people in there, Frank," I said. "It'll be dark, and we're in costume. We'll blend right in. Besides, no one will be paying close attention to the help."

"Okay," Frank whispered as we approached the door. "Let's do this."

A guy dressed in head-to-toe black stood planted at the door, checking names on a clipboard.

"Waiters?" he asked us, not looking up.

"At your service!" I said with a smile.

"Names?" he said.

I shot Frank a sideways glance. We had planned everything else except this part.

"Um—we're from the temp agency!" I blurted.

The guy finally looked up. "Temp agency?" he said.

"More like a catering and waitstaff agency," Frank explained quickly.

"Yeah!" Chet said. "It's called . . . Foods and Dudes."

"Who called your agency and asked for you?" the guy demanded.

Uh-oh.

"Um—it was Sierra!" I blurted. "Some girl named Sierra, I think. I'd have brought the job voucher, but I don't have pockets."

I held my breath. What if the guy went to get Sierra to confirm our story? But to my total relief he nodded and said, "Sierra does work for us. I can't be too careful, you realize. Everybody within twenty miles of Bayport wants to crash this party."

"We hear ya!" I told the guy as we filed past him into the kitchen.

"Look at this place!" Frank said as waiters and waitresses brushed past us, grabbing platters from long wooden tables.

"Look at the food!" Chet exclaimed.

A woman dressed in black hurried over to us. "Go ahead, guys," she said. "Grab some platters and make your rounds!"

Chet, Frank, and I darted to the food-filled table. As we took hold of the platters, we whispered our plans.

"Stay as close to each other as possible," Frank said. "Keep your eyes peeled for Colin without looking obvious."

"Check!" I said, lifting a round tray filled with mini pizzas.

Platters in hand, we followed the other waiters into the party hall. Our jaws must have hit the floor as we checked out the place.

"Whoa!" I cried. "What is this—a movie set?"

124

The huge hall was designed to look like an ancient Roman villa. There were tiled fountains, flaming torches, fake cedar trees, and—last but not least—mosaics on the wall and floor depicting Lindsay at different stages of her life.

"Sierra never told us about this," Frank said.

"There's a lot she didn't tell us," I said with a frown. "Now let's get to work before we get fired."

I'd taken about three steps forward when about a hundred hands reached for my tray.

"Is that cheese on the pizza soy or skim?" a girl with chandelier-size earrings asked.

"Can you bring out some oregano, dude?" a guy asked me. "The fresh kind, not the stuff in the jar."

"Will some mini quiche be coming out?" another girl asked. "Lindsay said there would be some."

I didn't know squat about mini quiche or the pizzas I was passing around, so I tried my best to wing some answers.

"I'll be back with the oregano," I told the guy, knowing full well I wouldn't.

The place pulsated with music as I continued on with my tray. I couldn't believe Lindsay had gotten the group Paradise Six to play her party—their latest song was number three on the charts!

"Excuse me, pardon me, excuse me," I kept saying as I squeezed through the mob of dancing and snacking guests. I spotted a few security guards, but they were busy eating and chatting at the buffet table.

Frank stopped next to me, holding a tray of barbecue wings. He saw me eyeing the guards and said, "Some security. Looks like Colin's plans to keep the police busy worked."

"Yeah, but where is Colin?" I asked.

Frank didn't answer. He was too busy staring ahead at something, his eyes wide.

When I saw who Frank was looking at, I gulped. Standing near the stage where the band was just finishing their tune was—

"Sierra," I muttered.

Sierra was staring too—at Frank, then at me. It wasn't long before her stare became an angry glare when she finally realized who we were.

"She probably figures we crashed the party," Frank murmured.

"What do we tell her if she comes over?" I asked.

Frank was about to say something when—*SMASH!!*

Screams filled the hall as something came crashing through a stained-glass window. The band stopped playing. Guests stared, stunned, at the shattered glass and what had caused it. It was a car tire!

The lights went up as Chet pushed his way over to Frank and me. The three of us watched as the tire rolled a few feet, then tipped on its side with a loud thump.

Frank, Chet, and I moved toward the tire. There, painted across the tire in red paint, was the word "Scaredevils"!

"Out of my way," a voice called out. "Out of my way, kids, please!"

I turned to see Sanford Peyton squeezing through the crowd. After staring at the tire, he shouted, "Is anybody hurt?"

When no one answered, he marched over to the security guards. "Don't just stand there," he said. "Go outside and get the criminals who did this!"

The guards and Sanford raced for the door. A half dozen Bayport Bijou employees raced to the broken glass with brooms and dustpans.

"We'd better go outside too," Frank said. "If this was Colin's doing, he's probably out there somewhere."

We were about to turn toward the door when the lights dimmed.

"Hail, good citizens!" Sierra's voice shouted.

I turned to see Sierra on the stage, a mike in her hand. The once-stunned guests were smiling again as they moved from the hurled tire to the stage.

The band struck a chord. All eyes were on Sierra as she said, "Please give it up for the most epic empress since Cleopatra—our Sweet Sixteen, Empress Lindsay!"

Guests seemed to forget about the broken window as they waved their arms in the air and chanted, "Lind-say! Lind-say! Lind-say!"

A pair of double doors burst wide open. Everyone went wild as four gladiators in full armor marched into the hall, carrying a throne balanced on two poles. Seated on the throne and waving to her adoring crowd was Lindsay—or should I say, Empress Lindsay.

The band struck up "Hotter Than Vesuvius" as the gladiators marched in a circle around the hall. The guys looked pretty authentic in their steel breastplates and heavy helmets, which covered three-quarters of their faces.

"Shouldn't we be outside looking for Colin?" Frank asked over the music.

Frank was right. But then I noticed something about the gladiators' costumes that didn't seem authentic at all.

"Hey, Frank?" I said slowly. "Since when do gladiators carry guns?"

NOT-SO-SUPER SWEET SIXTEEN

15

FRANK

UNS?" I ASKED, TRYING TO YELL OVER the music. "What guns?"

Joe gestured at the gladiators' sheaths as they marched by with Lindsay's throne. I saw what Joe was talking about. Instead of fake swords, these gladiators were packing heat!

"See what I mean?" Joe said to me.

I nodded slowly.

All I could see of the guns were the handles. The carved ivory told me they were antique.

"Joe," I whispered urgently. "Those are the kind of guns we saw at the Sylvesters'."

Chet was right behind us, listening in. "So what are you saying?" he asked.

"I'm saying one of those gladiators is Colin," I said, narrowing my eyes at the procession. "And he didn't come alone."

The parade of gladiators came to a sudden stop. Lindsay gasped as her throne jerked. Without warning, the gladiators released their grips on the throne, sending it to the floor with a heavy thud. Many of the guests gasped as Lindsay tumbled off the throne onto the floor.

"Hey!" she shrieked.

All four gladiators drew their guns. One pulled out a rifle, which he turned toward the band. "Shut up!" he shouted. "All of you!"

I didn't have to see beyond the heavy helmet to know it was Colin.

"Okay, what's going on?" a Bijou manager said as she squeezed through the crowd of guests. She took one look at the gun and paled. "I see."

Guests and staff stood frozen, too stunned to speak. The only one in the crowd who seemed cool was Sierra. With a small smile on her face, she joined the gladiators.

"Friends, Romans, countrymen, lend me your ears!" Colin shouted through his helmet. "Or better—lend me your bling-bling, watches, and phones!"

I glanced around for the guards, but they had gone outside to investigate the hurled tire. The smashed window must have been Colin's idea to get them out of the way.

"Frank, we've got to do something!" Joe said.

"Do what?" I shot back. "Those guns weren't part of our game plan!"

Two of the gladiators waved their weapons at the guests. One by one, they dropped their jewelry and electronics onto a third gladiator's shield, held out like a tray. The clinking sound of each item hitting the metal was chilling and infuriating.

Joe was right. We had to do something. And fast.

"Here's what I think we should do," I whispered to Joe and Chet. "It's not foolproof, but it's worth a shot."

"Shot?" Chet murmured. "Bad word choice, dude."

"Go on!" Joe urged me.

With one eye on the gladiators, I whispered my plan. "We wait until they come over to us. Chet, you knee the shield up into the guy's face. While that's going down, Joe and I will go for the guns."

"What about Colin over there?" Joe whispered. "He's got a gun too."

"Uh, like, a big gun!" Chet added.

A commotion broke out across the room. One guy was refusing to hand over his expensive-looking phone.

"Come on," Sierra shouted at him. "Hand it over!"

Lindsay pulled herself up off the floor and stared open-mouthed at Sierra.

"Wait a minute, Sierra," Lindsay said angrily. "You're in on this? Who are these guys?"

"Shut your mouth, birthday girl!" Colin shouted at Lindsay.

Lindsay planted her hands on her hips.

"Look, jerk," Lindsay shouted back. "I don't know who you are, but you're ruining my Sweet Sixteen!"

Colin threw back his helmeted head. "That's the idea, Linny," he said with a laugh.

"Wait a minute, I know that voice!" Lindsay said through gritted teeth. She ran up to him so they were inches apart, face to face. Colin threw off his helmet. "I knew it!" Lindsay exclaimed. "You guys, it's Colin Sylvester!"

Groans rose up from the crowd—until Colin pointed his rifle straight at Lindsay's head.

The crowd fell silent. A few guests sobbed softly while Lindsay froze with fear. Without moving a muscle, she uttered, "Don't shoot . . . please."

I knew we couldn't wait. We had to stop Colin now!

I saw Joe grab one of the flaming torches from its stand. I grabbed one too. Together we marched toward Colin and his menacing rifle.

"Drop the gun, Colin!" I demanded.

Colin turned away from Lindsay. When he saw us, he chuckled. "Well, if it isn't the boy detectives," he said. "I suppose you can fight with fire. Although I prefer firepower!"

Gasps filled the room as Colin aimed the rifle at Joe and me. I thrust my flaming torch at Colin. It didn't touch him, but he jumped, letting the gun drop from his hands.

Joe and I lunged for the rifle. We didn't get very far. . . .

"You guys, look out!" Lindsay shouted.

I glanced over my shoulder to see the other three gladiators moving toward us. Joe and I traded worried looks. Our torches might have been effective with Colin, but they were no match for three powerful guns coming our way!

I thought it was over, until I heard a loud, long creak. Looking up, I saw a fake tree beginning to tip over. I watched in shock as the tree came crashing down on the three gladiators, pinning them to the ground and knocking their guns from their hands.

"How did that happen?" Joe exclaimed.

We turned to see Chet at the base of the tree. Grinning triumphantly, he ran to grab the guns scattered on the floor. He was about to go for the last one when Sierra grabbed it first.

"Heads up!" Sierra shouted as she tossed the gun to Colin. He caught it with one hand, then turned it on us.

"Nice try, Hardys," Colin snapped. "But I win."

"Game's not over, Sylvester!" Joe shouted as he karate-kicked the gun out of Colin's hand. Colin stood stunned long enough for me to run around and grab him in a choke hold.

"Now game over!" I shouted.

But was it? From the corner of my eye, I saw one of the gladiators dragging himself out from under the tree. His eyes burned through his helmet as he slowly stood up. But before he could come after us . . .

"Stop right there!" a gruff voice boomed.

Joe and I whirled around to see Chief Olaf and his officers pushing through the crowd. Behind them, looking horrified, was Sanford Peyton.

I loosened my grip on Colin as the chief took hold of his arm.

"Nice work, boys," Chief Olaf grunted.

"Um . . . thanks," I said, surprised to hear the words coming out of the chief's mouth. "How did you know to come?"

"Are you kidding me?" Chief Olaf said. "Our station must have gotten a dozen calls and texts within the last fifteen minutes!"

I smiled as a slew of guests raised their cell phones triumphantly.

"Hey, Colin," Joe said with a laugh. "I guess not everybody handed over their fancy phones!"

Sanford had his arm draped around Lindsay's shoulder. "If only I'd been here to stop this," he said. "Why did I have to go outside?"

"You did fine, Mr. Peyton," Chief Olaf said. "You and the guards tracked down those Scaredevil punks. They're on their way to the station now."

Colin stared at the chief. "What did they tell you?" he demanded. "If they told you I robbed the party, they lied."

He pointed at Joe, Chet, then me. "Those are the guys who came with the guns. They're the ones you should be taking in!"

"Oh, blah, blah, blah, Colin," Lindsay said with a sigh.

She turned to Chief Olaf. "Colin and his friends snuck in here dressed as gladiators, with the help of Sierra, may I add. They're the ones who tried to rob us."

Colin's face glowed red as guests called out in agreement. I glanced at Sierra. She appeared to be muttering something to Lindsay through gritted teeth. I had a feeling it wasn't "Happy birthday!"

"Thank you, Miss Peyton," Chief Olaf said. "I'm sure we've got some Scaredevils at the station attesting to everything you said."

"Call my father!" Colin demanded as cuffs were put around his wrists. "I'm sure you can both work something out."

The chief shook his head. "Your dad's money won't help you this time, Colin," he said. "And I'm sure your dad won't be thrilled to know you were playing with his guns."

"Which were not loaded, by the way!" an officer holding the guns called over.

Colin really turned red now. No wonder the vintage guns hadn't gone off when they'd hit the floor.

"Let's hope your dad can afford the bail," Chief Olaf told Colin. "And I'd be interested in seeing some of those videos you and your friends starred in."

Joe folded his arms across his chest as he eyed Colin.

"Did you do it, Colin?" he asked. "Did you pay off those kids to keep the police away from the party?"

"What if I did?" Colin snapped. He turned his glare

toward Lindsay. "After the way she treated me, it's a small price to pay for revenge."

Lindsay stared at Colin as the chief led him out of the hall. I turned to see Sierra being led out too, along with the other gladiators, their helmets removed to reveal their faces.

"Sierra must have canceled the real gladiators and replaced them with Colin's friends," Joe figured.

"Man," I sighed, "did she have me fooled."

"She had us all fooled, Frank," Joe said. "But now the joke's on her."

"And on her psycho boyfriend," Chet added.

Sanford Peyton smiled at Joe, then at me. It was the first smile I'd seen from him yet.

"I'd like to thank you guys for your help," he said. "I'm just learning that you're quite the detectives."

"Don't forget our friend Chet," Joe said. "If he hadn't brought down that tree, who knows what would have happened?"

"Hey," Chet joked, wiggling his hand. "It's all in the wrist!"

This time Lindsay smiled. "I guess all three of you guys are gladiator material after all," she said. "Why don't you stay and hang with us?"

"Why?" Joe teased. "So we can serve mini quiche and hot wings?"

"No!" Lindsay laughed. "So you can party!"

She spun around, calling out to her friends, "Bayport High guys really rock—am I right?"

Their answer came in an earsplitting cheer. Chet shrugged and said, "Cool."

Paradise Six struck a chord as Lindsay jumped back on her throne. Waving both arms in the air, she shouted, "By order of your divine empress, let's get this party started . . . again!"

Some of the cops stuck around to return the stolen goods and make sure everybody was okay. As for Joe, Chet, and me—our job was done.

Joe grinned at me as we made a beeline for the dessert table. "You know, Frank," he said. "Those Bay Academy kids aren't so bad."

"With the exception of a few," I said. "Like maybe four or five?"

"What about those Scaredevils who go to our school?" Chet asked. "What do you think is going to happen to them?"

I shrugged. "They trashed Bayport for the money," I said. "Hopefully they'll fix it up. But that'll be up to the judge."

We stood in line for the designer birthday cake, sculpted to look like an ancient Roman temple. A model of Empress Lindsay chiseled from Rice Krispies treats waved from the top.

"You got to see it to believe it," Joe said, chuckling.

"Speaking of believing," I said, "do you think the kids at school will believe we just battled an army of gladiators with nothing but torches and karate kicks?"

"Sure they will!" Chet said. He pulled Joe's tablet from his waist pouch and held it high. "And if they don't, I've got it all on tape!"

READ ON

FOR A SNEAK PEEK
OF THE NEXT MYSTERY IN THE
HARDY BOYS ADVENTURES:

THE VANISHING GAME

FRANK

ID YOU KNOW THAT COTTON CANDY depends heavily on the molecular construction of sugar?" I asked brightly, grabbing a hunk of my brother Joe's fluffy pink confection and popping it into my mouth. "The cotton candy machine uses centrifugal force to spin hot sugar so quickly and cool it so rapidly, the sugar doesn't have time to recrystallize!"

My date—or so I'd been told, because she didn't seem super attached to me—Penelope Chung, rolled her eyes. "That's fascinating, Frank," she said, shooting a glare at her best friend, Daisy Rodriguez, who was Joe's date and the glue barely holding our foursome together. "Please tell me more about molecules. Or force times acceleration. Or the atomic properties of *fun*."

Joe coughed loudly, grabbing my shoulder and pulling me close enough to hear him mutter, "Ixnay on the ience-scay."

I couldn't help it. Joe is always telling me science isn't romantic, but *come on*. Isn't "romance" itself a scientific concept? Attraction, biology, all that stuff?

Daisy smiled, a little too enthusiastically. "Shall we head over to the G-Force?" she asked, looking hopefully from Penelope and me to Joe. "My dad said the first ride would be at eight o'clock. And it's just about quarter of."

"Yes!" Penelope cried before Joe or I could respond, grabbing Daisy's arm and pulling her ahead of us toward Funspot's new ride, G-Force. Penelope leaned close to Daisy's ear, and while I couldn't hear what she was saying, her tone did not sound warm.

Joe met my eye and sighed.

"I don't think she likes me," I told him.

Joe just shook his head and patted my back. "I think your powers of detection are dead-on true, bro."

We started walking. "Sorry," I said. "I know you're really into Daisy."

Joe nodded. "It's okay, man," he said, holding out his cotton candy for me to take another hunk. "I just don't think you're Penelope's type."

I nodded. "But it's pretty cool that we get to be some of the first people to check out G-Force, right?"

"*Very* cool," Joe agreed.

G-Force was the new, premiere attraction at Funspot,

a small amusement park that had been a staple of Bayport summers for generations, but had been getting more and more run-down over the years. Last fall, Daisy's dad, Hector, had used their entire family's savings to buy the park from its longtime owner, Doug Spencer, who had fallen on hard times. Hector wanted to build Funspot into a top-tier amusement park—the kind of place people would drive hours to visit. His first step toward making that happen had been to install G-Force.

The ride was a new creation of Greg and Derek Piperato, better known as the Piperato Brothers—*the* hip new architects of premiere amusement rides all over the world. They built the HoverCoaster for Holiday Gardens in Copenhagen, the Loop-de-Loco for Ciudad de Jugar in Barcelona, and the ChillTaser for Bingo Village in Orlando, right here in the USA. These guys are seriously awesome at what they do. They know their physics, they know their architecture, and they keep coming up with new ideas to revolutionize the amusement industry.

They don't work cheap, though. According to Daisy, Hector had to take out a major loan to afford G-Force. And unfortunately, right after Hector signed the contracts—Funspot had exclusive rights to the ride for five years—Daisy's mom had been laid off from her job as a manager at some big bank in New York City. If Daisy and her family had hoped Funspot would be successful before, now their whole future was riding on the park's success.

"Wow," Joe breathed as we turned a corner, and there it was: G-Force!

For weeks, Hector had paid for advertisements on all the local radio stations: "Come to Funspot to ride G-Force! What does it do? You'll have to ride it to find out . . . but one thing's for sure"—here the voice got deep and creepy— *"you'll never be the same!"*

I had been sure that seeing the attraction would be a disappointment. I mean, how could you live up to that ad? Put aside the basic scientific impossibilities of its promises (*Never be the same?* What, would it change your molecular structure?); it was hard to imagine a ride so impressive that it could stand up to weeks of wondering what it might look like. But the structure in front of me was, in a word, *awesome*. It was sleek and silver and had the curved, aerodynamic shape of a spaceship.

"Wow," I echoed, pointing at it like a kindergartner. "That thing is cool!"

Joe looked confused, then followed my gaze and nodded. "Oh, sure. It does look cool. But I was talking about the crowd—check it out!"

I looked around. Joe was right. The line coiled around several times before stretching all the way from the ride, through the "kiddie park" (where Joe and I had spent countless hours on the helicopter ride as kids), down the row of food stands, and nearly to the parking lot. When we'd arrived at the park hours earlier, it hadn't been nearly as long.

But it looked like all those radio advertisements worked!

"Looks like a lot of people want to be forced—g-forced!" I said, smiling, as Daisy and Penelope slowed their pace and we caught up to them.

Daisy looked thrilled. "I guess so!" she said, looking around at the crowd like she couldn't believe it. "It looks like the whole student body of Bayport High is here!"

Joe nodded, surveying the huge line. "We—uh—don't have to wait in that, do we?"

"Of course not." Daisy smiled and shook her head, gallantly taking Joe by the arm. "Follow me, mister. The four of us are skipping this line. It pays to have friends in high places!"

Penelope glanced at me warily, but we both fell into step behind Joe and Daisy. She'd been right: The line was crowded with our classmates from Bayport High. Some smiled and waved at Daisy as we passed, or called out their congratulations. But as we walked by one sullen-looking group of boys, a dark-haired kid stepped out and blocked Daisy's path.

"Well, well, well," he said, giving the four of us a not-very-friendly once-over. "What have we here? The kings and queens of Funspot?"

As Joe shot her a questioning glance, Daisy frowned at the kid. "Let us by, Luke."

He didn't move, but met her gaze without a smile. "Is this your new *boyfriend*?" He scowled at Joe.

Joe stepped forward, holding out his hand. "Hey, man . . ."

But Daisy just shook her head. "What do you care?" she asked, looking from the boy to his chuckling friends in line. "Joe, Frank, this is my *ex*-boyfriend, Luke."

"Emphasis on *ex*," Penelope piped up, stepping forward to give Luke a withering stare.

Luke glared at Penelope for a moment, but her words seemed to wound him, and he quickly looked down before stepping aside. Daisy hesitated for a moment, then turned around and walked briskly past. Penelope followed, her head held high, and Joe and I began to follow.

"Hey!" Luke called after us when we were a few feet away, and Daisy was almost at the ride. "Congrats on the turnout tonight!"

Daisy paused, turning slowly to look back at him.

Luke's expression turned to an ugly smirk. "Guess you can go to college after all!" he shouted, loud enough for the crowd to hear. His group of friends erupted into loud chuckles. Daisy cringed.

Joe was furious. I could tell he was upset on Daisy's behalf and would have loved to teach him a lesson. But instead he pulled out his phone. "Smile," he said to Luke, snapping a picture.

Luke was taken aback. "What did you do that for?" he demanded angrily.

Joe just smiled. "When we go to security and tell them a

group is being rowdy and disruptive, this way they'll know who to look for."

Luke glared at Joe. I had to smile. I seriously doubted Joe had any intention of going to security—but the look on Luke's face made it clear he didn't know that.

Joe touched Daisy's arm. "Shall we?" he asked, gesturing to the ride.

Daisy looked like she wasn't sure what to do. Penelope shot Luke another icy look, then moved toward Daisy. "Let's go, Daze," she said, pushing her forward. "He's such a jerk."

After a moment, Daisy moved on, and the three of us followed close behind.

At the head of the line, an older, gruff-looking guy with ruddy skin and dark hair and beard stood behind a narrow metal gate. He looked at Daisy and nodded. "Miss." Without another word, he opened the gate, and the four of us walked through.

"Thanks, Cal," Daisy said, smiling brightly. "Do I have time to quickly show my friends the ride before it starts?"

Cal nodded, not making eye contact. He locked the gate, then led the four of us up a metal gangplank toward the shining, brushed-chrome ride. A small rectangular door was embedded in the side, and Cal easily pulled it open, gesturing for us to enter. Behind us, people were hooting and hollering, clearly eager to get onto the ride themselves.

Inside, small purple lights recessed into the ceiling and

walls provided just enough light to make out a circle of huge, cushy seats, each with a sturdy restraining bar, surrounding an open center. I strained to see the ceiling, the floor, anything that would give a hint to what the ride actually *did*—but it was too dark.

"So . . . what does it do?" I asked Cal, who had paused in front of a bank of seats.

He turned to me and smiled. In the low purple light I could just make out that he was missing several teeth. He laughed, a low, raspy sound.

"I guess you'll just have to ride it and find out, won't you?" he asked. Then he nodded at the door. "Let's get you strapped in."

Daisy and Penelope smiled and eagerly chose seats next to each other. As Cal was securing the restraints around each of them, I glanced at my brother. I thought he looked pale.

"Are you okay?" I whispered. His eyes were darting around the ride nervously.

He bit his lip. "What do you think the ads meant," he whispered, "when they said, 'You'll never be the same'?"

I opened my mouth to answer, but Joe immediately held up his hand to shush me. "Never mind," he whispered. "I don't want Daisy to hear."

At that moment, Cal finished strapping in Penelope and looked back at us. Joe smiled eagerly—I mean, I guess it was supposed to look eager, but to me it looked kind of insane—and walked over to the seat next to Daisy. As he got strapped in, I settled into the seat next to Penelope.

She looked at me warily. "Great," she said tonelessly, "we get to ride together."

I nodded. "There was a rumor on Amusementgeeks.com that this ride will send you into another dimension," I told her, "but of course that's scientifically impossible."

"Good to know," she said, and turned back to Daisy.

Cal came over and quickly strapped me in, placing two restraining belts over my shoulders and clicking a wide metal bar into place just inches from my stomach. He jiggled the bar a little to make sure it was tight, then, apparently satisfied, turned and exited the ride without a word.

"So, have you test-driven the ride?" Joe asked Daisy, breaking the silence.

She shook her head. "I wish," she said with a sigh. "But my dad's agreement with the Piperato Brothers was very specific. *No one*—except the test subjects they used when they were designing the ride, I guess—gets to ride G-Force before its official opening." She checked her watch. "Which happens—wow—in about three minutes!"

Before any of us could reply, the door opened again, and eager riders from the line began filing in, oohing and aahing, straining to get a good look at the ride's interior. They milled around and selected seats, and after a minute or so, Cal entered and began to strap all the riders in.

"So, Daisy," Brian Mullin, one of the football players, spoke up. "Is this ride going to change my life, or what?"

Daisy chuckled. "You know what the ads say, Brian," she replied, deepening her voice. *"You'll never be the same."*

Brian snickered. "Well, I hope I come out taller."

Cal was just finishing strapping in the last rider, and as we all laughed at Brian's joke, he glanced around at all of us, then nodded. "Enjoy the ride," he said, not smiling, and then exited through the tiny door. It closed behind him, and the inside of the ride darkened even further.

Everyone grew quiet as we waited for the ride to begin. In the quiet, I picked up a weird clicking sound—like someone tapping their fingernails against a hard surface. I looked to my right, where the sound was coming from. Penelope was looking around too, seeming to hear it, and Daisy glanced at her and frowned, then turned to Joe.

"Are your *teeth chattering*?" she asked.

But Joe didn't get a chance to answer—at that very moment, the purple lights clicked off and we were immersed in darkness. A huge *whoosh* emanated from the floor—probably the ride's engine cranking up. Then a loud guitar chord sounded: I recognized it as the beginning of "Beautiful," a rock song that was climbing the charts. The song started up, and then suddenly we were moving—suddenly we were moving *really fast*! The circle of seats orbited faster and faster around the center, and I could feel the centrifugal force pushing me against the back of the seat. My head slammed back into the headrest, and it felt like the skin of my face was tightening, being pulled back by the force of the revolutions.

People began screaming, and suddenly the darkness was cut by a bright white light. I could make out the riders on the other side of the circle grimacing and beaming, screaming in fear and pleasure. Then the light cut out, then on again—a strobe light, making the whole ride look like it was in stop-motion.

The ride seemed to slow, and then suddenly the seats rose into the air. I gasped, exhilarated by the sudden motion. Just as quickly as they'd risen, though, they plunged down, farther, I think, than we'd been when the ride started. The strobe lights changed, suddenly, so that instead of bright white light, we saw neon images projected on the riders across from us—symbols, photographs of beautiful nature scenes, crying babies, an old woman smiling. The ride kept spinning, ascending, descending, but as hard as I tried, I couldn't keep track of all its motions. The scientist in me had wanted to break down exactly what G-Force did, but in the end, I just couldn't. The experience of the ride took over, and I screamed and laughed with everyone else, feeling totally exhilarated.

After some time—it could have been seconds or it could have been hours—the ride spun around again, gluing us all back in our seats. I closed my eyes as the revolutions slowed, and the music began to fade. Slower, slower, slower still we circled, until finally I felt the ride click into its resting position. I opened my eyes as the purple lights kicked on again, illuminating the ride with dim light.

Everyone looked like they'd been tumble dried. Hair stuck out in all directions, clothes were all rumpled, expressions dazed. But as we all looked at one another, not sure how to capture the experience, suddenly Brian Mullin began to clap slowly. The girl on his right joined in, and after a few seconds, so did everyone else on the ride.

"That was AWESOME!" Brian shouted.

His words seemed to give everyone else permission to speak too.

"That was AMAZING. . . ."

"Unreal . . ."

"I've never felt anything like that."

"Omigosh, I want to ride that, like, *ten* more times!"

I looked over at Daisy, who looked a little dazed herself, but a smile was creeping slowly to her lips. Joe (who looked less pale now) smiled at her and took her hand, giving it a little squeeze.

"Looks like Funspot's new main attraction is a hit," I heard him whisper to her.

But as everyone seemed to be giving their personal review of the ride, an increasingly concerned voice broke through the din.

"Kelly?"

Penelope sat up, grinning, and patted Daisy's shoulder. "Good job, Hector," she said. "I think he bought a winner!"

"Kelly?"

I looked across the ride, where the voice was coming from.

People were gradually stopping their own conversations, turning their attention to the spot where a girl about our age struggled against the restraints, stretching her neck to look around.

"Kelly? KELLY!"

The girl let out a sob.

"Oh no!" she cried. "No, no, no! Where is she?"

That's when I caught sight of the seat next to her.

"My sister *disappeared*!"

It was empty. And the restraints that should have held Kelly in place had been cut.

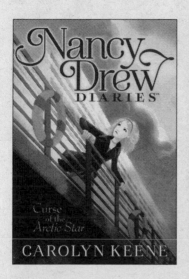
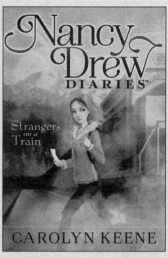

The truth is always closer than you think. . . .

JULIA PLATT LEONARD

COLD CASE

The truth
is always closer
than you think.

EBOOK EDITION ALSO AVAILABLE

From Aladdin
KIDS.SimonandSchuster.com